A Duke's Daughters –
The Elbury Bouquet - Book 2

Clean Regency Romance

A VIXEN FOR A VISCOUNT

Arietta Richmond

ARIETTA RICHMOND

Dreamstone Publishing © 2019

www.dreamstonepublishing.com

ISBN-13: 978-1-925915-17-4

DISCLAIMER

This is a work of fiction. Names, characters, places, organisations, events, and incidents are either products of the author's imagination or used fictitiously.

ARIETTA RICHMOND

DEDICATION

For everyone who had the grace to be patient while this book, and every other book that I have written, was coming into existence, who provided cups of tea, and food, when the writing would not let me go, and endured countless times being asked for opinions.

For the readers who inspire me to continue writing, by buying my books! Especially for those of you who have taken the time to email me, or to leave reviews, and tell me what you love about my books, and what you'd like to see more of – thank you – I'm listening. I hope that you enjoy this new series (which features some appearances by old favourite characters from the His Majesty's Hounds series), just as much as my other books.

For my growing team of beta readers and advance reviewers – it's thanks to you that others can enjoy these books in the best presentation possible!

And for all the writers of Regency Historical Romance, whose books I read, who inspired me to write in this fascinating period.

TABLE OF CONTENTS

Books by Arietta Richmond

His Majesty's Hounds

Claiming the Heart of a Duke

Intriguing the Viscount

Giving a Heart of Lace

From Soldier Spy to Lord (contains the first three books in one volume)

Being Lady Harriet's Hero

Enchanting the Duke

Redeeming the Marquess

Finding the Duke's Heir

Winning the Merchant Earl

Healing Lord Barton

Kissing the Duke of Hearts

Loving the Bitter Baron

Falling for the Earl

Rescuing the Countess

Betting on a Lady's Heart

Attracting the Spymaster

Courting a Spinster for Christmas

Restoring the Earl's Honour

The Regency Scandals Series

The Gift of a Christmas Scandal

Lady Mariel's Scandalous Love (coming soon)

Christmas with *That* Duke (coming soon)

Other Books

The Scottish Governess (coming soon)

The Earl's Reluctant Fiancée (coming soon)

The Crew of the Seadragon's Soul Series,
(coming soon - a set of 10 linked novels)

The Nettlefold Chronicles
The Duke and the Spinster
To Dance with the Dangerous Duke
A Duke in Autumn (coming soon)
A Christmas Bride for the Duke (coming soon)

A Duke's Daughters – The Elbury Bouquet
A Spinster for a Spy (Lily)
A Vixen for a Viscount (Hyacinth)
A Bluestocking for a Baron (Rose) (coming soon)
A Diamond for a Duke (Camellia) (coming soon)
A Minx for a Merchant (Primrose) (coming soon)
An Enchantress for an Earl (Violet) (coming soon)
A Maiden for a Marquess (Iris) (coming soon)
A Heart for an Heir (Thorne) (coming soon)

The Derbyshire Set
A Gift of Love (Prequel short story)
A Devil's Bargain (Prequel short story - coming soon)
The Earl's Unexpected Bride
The Captain's Compromised Heiress
The Viscount's Unsuitable Affair
The Derbyshire Set, Omnibus Edition, Volume 1
(contains the first three books in a single volume.)
The Count's Impetuous Seduction
The Rake's Unlikely Redemption
The Marquess' Scandalous Mistress
The Derbyshire Set, Omnibus Edition, Volume 2
(contains the second three books in a single volume.)
A Remembered Face (Bonus short story – coming soon)
The Marchioness' Second Chance
A Viscount's Reluctant Passion (coming soon)
Lady Theodora's Christmas Wish
The Duke's Improper Love (coming soon)

ARIETTA RICHMOND

CHAPTER ONE

Lord Kevin Loughbridge leant casually against the wall of the ballroom, watching the swirl of people move about the room. He had been cultivating an air of what he thought of as 'stylish ennui' of late – as if the entire world was rather dull, and hardly worth his consideration. Young women seemed to find it both attractive and daunting – which made them less likely to pursue him.

Not that he objected to being found attractive, but he did object to insipid conversation – which was all that most of the young ladies seemed able to offer. In the face of the strong characters of both of his sisters, and of his brother-in-law's sisters, all of the fluttering hopefuls seemed faded, pale imitations of real people. Well, not quite all of them.

His eyes fell on a group of people who had just arrived, and were making their way across the ballroom towards, if he was not mistaken, his sister Nerissa, where she stood with her husband, the Duke of Melton. It was the Duke and Duchess of Elbury, their seven daughters, and their son.

None of that family were as faded and insipid as most. His gaze went to one in particular of the daughters. Lady Hyacinth Gardenbrook was tall, her hair a dark blonde shade that was almost brown, like the pale rich tone of the caramels that their cook had made when he was a boy. On the surface, she was everything that a young woman of the *ton* should be – immaculately presented, dressed in a stunning gown of a blue that was an echo of her name, with pearls and tiny blue flowers twined into her uplifted hair.

But what made her interesting was her reputation. At one and twenty, this was her third Season, and she was, like the rest of her sisters, as yet unmarried. The whispered wisdom amongst the gentlemen laid that fact squarely upon the sharpness of her tongue. She was renowned for having a frighteningly acid wit, and the ability to crush a gentleman with a few words, all whilst still being exquisitely polite.

That was, he thought, about as far from the insipid faded conversation of most women as he could imagine getting. As a result, most of the men he knew avoided any significant conversation with her – they danced with her, still half tempted by the size of her dowry, but none lasted long as a suitor. Thus, she intrigued him. So he had studied her, whenever he had seen her, since the start of this Season. Tonight, he rather thought that he was ready to put himself into the path of danger – to ask her to dance, and to see if he could survive the resultant conversation unscathed.

He thought that he could – although that may be a delusion – for he had learned much of her, by observation. No matter what was whispered of her, he was quite certain that she was kind at heart, and ferocious in defence of those she cared about.

In an odd way, she reminded him of his brother-in-law's mother – the Dowager Duchess of Melton – who did her best to be autocratic and overbearing, but loved her children and friends dearly, and always let them have their way, in the end. He had never met another young woman who took such an attitude to life – and he suspected that he might never do so.

With a deep breath, he straightened from his indolent pose against the wall, and set off across the ballroom towards her.

<<<< O >>>>

Lady Hyacinth Gardenbrook smiled at no-one in particular, her face set in what she thought of as her 'social event mask'. As they crossed the ballroom towards the group of people around the Duke and Duchess of Melton, she watched her sister out of the corner of her eye. Lily was gazing directly at Lord Canterford, as if no-one else existed. It had been that way for a month or so now. Hyacinth wished her well of it, but was a little disappointed in her sister – she had never expected Lily to succumb to the doe eyed adoration of a gentleman – not like all of the other ninnies that populated society Balls. But it seemed that she had.

Really, she should have expected it – Lily had been surrounded by hopeful suitors for three years now – it had to happen eventually. Around them, people moved and circulated – many greeting their family as they crossed the room. The gentlemen all paid attention to one or another of her sisters, but not really to Hyacinth. She repressed a sigh. She knew why they barely attended to her – she had a reputation as something of a shrew, a reputation that she had, mostly, earned. Why were so many men afraid of hearing the truth of things?

She did not know. But she had discovered, very soon after coming out into society, that they were, that speaking what seemed obvious truth to her was seen as sharp, and rude, by most of them. Especially if it pricked the bubble of their own conceit. She had tried, at least at first, to temper her comments, to phrase them more politely, even to hold her tongue. It had not worked. Her comments had become, if anything, sharper, just more politely packaged, so that it was harder for people to take offence, directly.

Two years ago, she had found it amusing, in a rather dark fashion. Now, she was beginning to find it a cause for secret despair. She did not, she had realised, wish to spend her life as an eccentric spinster, like their great-aunt Petunia. But that seemed more and more likely as time passed, for unless she could find a man who was not driven away by her pointed observations of the world, there was no other way that she could end.

For a moment, even in the midst of the busy ballroom, she allowed herself to daydream, to imagine what a man might be like, who found her sharpness of wit and observation interesting, rather than threatening – a man who might see who she was, as a whole person, rather than just an astringent voice, with an eye to his failings. She repressed a snort of self-deprecating laughter – that would never do at a Ball – for surely she imagined a paragon, who did not exist. She really must try again, to seem less dragonish, and more demure. She nearly snorted again – for that was an impossible thing to ask of her – she had already tried and failed so many times.

As they arrived at the group near the Duke of Melton, another man joined the party. A man she did not remember seeing before.

He seemed unexceptionable – quite tall, well put together, with dark reddish-brown hair and rich brown eyes. For a moment, she met those eyes, and shivered – he did not look away. After a moment, she did, cursing herself for the weakness, even as she excused herself with the fact that to stare would be rude – especially with a man she had not been introduced to. Now that she thought on it, perhaps she had seen him before – but he had always held himself aloof, speaking to few people, and mainly watching what went on around him.

Hyacinth found herself wanting to know more of him.

She started as the Duchess spoke.

"Ladies, may I make known to you my brother, Lord Kevin Loughbridge? Kevin, this is Lady Lily, Lady Hyacinth, Lady Rose, Lady Camellia, Lady Primrose, Lady Violet and Lady Iris Gardenbrook."

Lord Kevin bowed to each in turn, and spoke to all of them.

"I am delighted to meet you all. My sister has mentioned you, and I can now confirm that you are quite as beautiful as she reported."

The younger girls giggled a little, and Hyacinth glared at them, causing them to subside, then brought her eyes back to Lord Kevin. He was watching her. And his expression was not at all what she expected. He had seen her glare at the others, that much was obvious, yet he seemed amused, more than anything else. She was not used to being regarded as amusing. Did he know nothing of her reputation? Instinctively, she spoke, without prior thought.

"You flatter outrageously, Lord Kevin."

Internally she winced. This was not a good beginning, if she was trying to be more socially astute. Beside her, Rose looked a little shocked at her bald statement. Let her be shocked. It was said now, and Hyacinth could not but be herself, no matter how hard she tried to be otherwise.

"But surely, stating the truth cannot be truly remarked as flattery. Flattery, by its nature, involves some exaggeration, or even falsehood, and neither was present in my words."

The world spun. He was debating her contention, not being offended by it. No man had ever done that before.

"I concede that your definition is, perhaps, correct, Lord Kevin – but surely you cannot believe us to all be equally beautiful, to permit such a broad generalisation?"

Her sisters were now all watching her as if she was mad – all except Lily, who was lost in Lord Canterford's gaze. She did not care, perhaps she was mad, but if so, it was a madness she did not wish to be free of.

"Perhaps, but, if you examine my words, you will discover that I have left myself with an escape clause. For I said 'that you are quite as beautiful as my sister reported' – and you do not know, at this point, what Nerissa actually said to me…"

He was right. Hyacinth felt the foundations of her world spin again. Not only was he debating her contentions, he was winning. It was insupportable, and utterly delightful at the same time.

"You are, I begin to perceive, a most devious man, Lord Kevin. And this is a most unusual, and refreshing, conversation, if I may say so."

"I might, perhaps, admit that you have the right of it. And it is indeed." His eyes were laughing at her! She was, for the first time in her adult life, at a loss for what to say. He saved her from an embarrassing silence. "Lady Hyacinth, I believe that the dancing is about to begin – will you grant me the honour of this dance?"

She blinked, stunned. After that conversation, he wanted to dance with her? Every other man she had ever met would have fled by now, sure that she was an irredeemable shrew, with far too many opinions for a woman. There were no words, but she found herself placing her hand on his proffered arm, in concert with a regal inclination of her head. She was quite sure that he stifled a laugh, as he led her to the dance floor in the wake of Lily and Lord Canterford.

<<<< O >>>>

Kevin was enjoying himself – far more than he had expected to. She was a delight – utterly different from the pale faded flutterers, and so confident in her approach to the world. He had rarely met a woman so willing to speak her mind. And he was discovering that he liked that, that the removal of all need to analyse each word for hidden meanings and implications was restful, allowing conversation to simply be a process of two minds dissecting an idea, or a point of contention.

In the back of his mind he wondered if he was mad, to think so – most of his friends would say that he was, that no good could come of a woman having opinions, and being self-determining – but he rather thought that his sisters disproved that idea. Lady Hyacinth simply confirmed for him that it was actually possible to have a real conversation with a woman not of his family.

He was particularly pleased when his request that she dance with him produced stunned silence – he suspected that was a rare occurrence for Lady Hyacinth. But she allowed him to lead her to the floor, and he stifled his laughter – truly, he had no wish to mock her – challenge her, perhaps, but never mock.

They stepped into place in the line, and the dance began, the turning about other couples in intricate steps leaving little room for conversation. So he simply watched her instead, enjoying the surety of her movements, the unconscious elegance of her, as she flowed through the dance. Apparently, she found his silence unnerving, for as the dance brought them back together, she spoke. And she surprised him again.

"I perceive, Lord Kevin, that I must ask you a question, for my own piece of mind. I am quite, quite certain that you have heard my reputation, as rather a shrew, spoken of by various gentlemen. Yet here you are, dancing with me, after that conversation. So – are you doing this because a friend dared you to beard the dragon? Or actually because you want to?"

CHAPTER TWO

She had surprised him, she knew it, from the fleeting glimpse she had of his expression, just before the dance spun them apart again. Surprised, not shocked. Then they came back together, and he rendered her speechless – for he laughed – he actually had the temerity to laugh at her words!

Whilst she was adjusting to the shock of that, and schooling her face into a steady expression, he spoke – it was quiet, half whispered into her ear as they turned about one another, but the tone of it was warm enough to send shivers through her.

"My dear Lady Hyacinth, I can assure you that I am doing 'this' because I want to. None of my friends are fool enough to believe that daring me would make me do anything but ignore them. And I do not, at all, believe you a dragon – you are far too young and comely to be named for a scaly, fire breathing monster. Nor would I call you a shrew – nasty bitey little things they are. Perhaps, though, a vixen I might allow – cunning, sharp toothed, but most judicious in the use of those teeth."

She continued to turn, his words rather dizzying.

Taking a deep breath, she summoned all of her long practice at delivering set downs, and attempted one – yet there was a disturbing part of her mind which was not at all sure that such a thing would work, with this man.

"Dear me, Lord Kevin, I do believe that your skill at flattery and correct social conversation has failed you. For I cannot see any light in which comparing a lady to a vixen might be considered a compliment."

He laughed again, obviously unworried by her censure. He really was a most unusual gentleman!

"You can't? Are you sure? Would you not rather be compared to something quick and clever like a fox, than to something so insipid and overused as a flower, or the stars, or pearls and diamonds? I cannot see you as anything so bland as the stuff of most common compliments."

The dance spun them apart again, and Hyacinth felt flushed and breathless, her mind whirling – what could she say to that! They came back together, and she met his eyes.

"Perhaps I would prefer to be the dragon. For surely, to be large and frightening has its benefits – I doubt that anyone wishes to argue with a dragon – but people regularly hunt foxes."

"You do have a point, my Lady. But still, legend has it that people hunt dragons too – at least knights brave enough to be foolish do. And a dragon is rather large and obvious – a fox finds it far easier to hide when it wishes to, and slip past all but the keenest observers. That is a skill to be respected. And a skill which I believe I have seen you apply, many times."

"Do you imply, Lord Kevin, that you have been... observing me?"

He smiled, and a shiver went through her again.

"It would be most ungentlemanly of me to admit such a thing. But perhaps I can say that I have found it... difficult to *not* notice you..."

Her heart beat unaccountably fast, even allowing for the energetic movements that the dance required, and she pondered his words as the music finally drew to a close. They spun through the final turn, and to a halt, facing each other. Hyacinth lifted her fan, and flipped it open, needing the distraction. His deep brown eyes drew her in, and it took her a moment to realise that he held out his arm, awaiting the moment when she would place her hand upon it. She did so, annoyed with herself, and he began to lead her back to her family.

"I do believe that you flatter again, Lord Kevin. But I will admit to being intrigued – for you imply that, knowing my reputation, and having observed the... manner... in which I tend to treat most gentlemen, you are yet still here, by your own choice, subjecting yourself to my sharp toothed conversation."

"You have, my Lady, the right of it. That is, exactly, the situation," they had reached the cluster of her sisters, and he turned to face her, bowing, "a situation which I find enough to my liking that I intend, with your permission, to repeat it, at future events such as this."

How did he do this to her? How did he unmoor the foundations of her world so easily?

Yet... there was only one possible answer to his words.

"I will grant you that permission, my Lord. We shall see how well you weather the storm when next we meet."

He bowed again, his fingers pressing hers, perhaps just a tiny amount more than might be socially correct, then he released her, and turned and walked away. Against her conscious will, her eyes followed him.

"My dear sister, how enlightening! I do believe that you have just provided me with a reason to tease you, rather than allowing Lily to bear the full weight of my amusement."

Hyacinth turned, schooling her face into absolute calm.

"Dear brother, tease me? I fear that you have become addled in your mind. What possible cause could you have to tease me?"

Thorne Gardenbrook, Marquess of Wildenhall, took his sister's arm, and led her towards the refreshment tables.

"Hyacinth, if you think that, for a moment, I am going to be deceived by that innocent expression, then you are far more foolish than I believed you. For this evening, I have seen something I never thought to see – you, dancing with a man, gazing at him with rapt attention, and, at least twice, rendered temporarily speechless. I can think of but one possible reason for such a reaction."

Hyacinth took the glass of orgeat he handed her, and sipped, wondering how on earth she might cause her brother to forget what he had seen.

Chester House felt empty. His parents rarely came to London now, especially since all of the drama the previous year with Maria, and the death of her husband. Now that was past, and things had settled down a lot, they stayed at Chester Park with Maria, as she began to rebuild her life. Which rebuilding was proceeding rather well, from Kevin's perspective, as it looked almost certain that she would marry Viscount Wareham, who was brother to the Duke of Melton, and also a long term friend.

But it left Chester House echoingly empty.

Kevin took his brandy to the library, and settled in front of the fire. It might be spring, but the evenings were still rather cool, and the warmth was welcome. As he stared into the flames, he replayed the events of the evening in his mind. Lady Hyacinth Gardenbrook was fascinating – there was no other word for it. One dance, one conversation, and he found himself looking forward to seeing her again.

He almost laughed at the thought – his acquaintances in society would deem him quite mad for that – for they were all firmly convinced that she was an irredeemable shrew. A fact which had less to do with Lady Hyacinth's actual character, and more to do with his acquaintances' lack of mental and verbal agility, in Kevin's opinion. When might he see her again? There were Balls and soirees most nights now, as the Season was in full swing, so the chances were good that they might both be in attendance at a number of events in the week ahead.

He frowned, staring at the flames, but seeing something else entirely. Could he afford to stay in London for the rest of the week? He needed to go back to Chester Park, for a few days at least, and soon.

It wasn't that his parents would expect him to leave London, but more that he felt that he needed to. There was something not right at Chester Park, beyond the things that Maria still struggled with. He was sure that his father was hiding something from him.

Each time he went home, his father seemed more careworn, and quieter, as if he lacked the strength to do as much as he had been in the habit of doing. But he said nothing of it, and Kevin was loath to push him. Still, more and more, he wanted to be close by, so that he could deal with whatever happened, if anything did.

He sipped the brandy, and made a decision – another four days in London, which was at least two possible chances to see Lady Hyacinth, and then he would go to Chester Park for a week. Perhaps, if he was persistent enough, he might get his father to speak of whatever was wrong – he could not ask outright, but surely, with enough chances, his father would tell him? But then again, Lord Chester was, if nothing else, a very stubborn man.

<<<< O >>>>

Hyacinth sat in her bed, a half-eaten breakfast tray on the table beside her. On the mornings after a Ball, she liked to stay late in bed and, once her breakfast had been delivered, she chose not to be disturbed by anyone until she was ready. In a family as large as the Gardenbrooks, such time to oneself was precious – and each of her sisters had their own habits of ensuring personal time too.

What Hyacinth did with that personal time was something that was just for her – and almost certainly not something that the rest of the family would expect.

The journal in her hands was old, bound in now worn dark red-toned leather, and rather battered – it had been given to her when she was a child, and the first few pages were graced with extremely poor illustrations of what were supposed to be hyacinth flowers, done in blotchy watercolours. She had been so frustrated by her inability to render them well, all those years ago, that she had refused to put her name on the journal, and had simply put it away, and ignored it.

It had stayed in the back corner of a drawer in her dressing room, until two years earlier, when she had discovered it again, by accident. Since then, it had filled a far different purpose from its original use. For when she had come out, she had found her head full of observations of the people around her in society – observations which she most rapidly discovered were not to be spoken aloud, to anyone. But she could not help doing the observing.

So she had taken the journal, and begun to record her thoughts about them all, after each event that she attended. It had become a soothing ritual – the morning after an event, she would take her breakfast in bed and write in the journal, using a sharpened pencil – for spilling ink on the bed was a risk that she chose not to take. What she wrote was an unmodified version of her observations from the previous evening – all sharp and scathing, and baldly delivering the truth of the people who had attended, rather than the socially acceptable version of events.

If she was not permitted to say what she thought in society, then she was most certainly going to do so in the privacy of her own journal. Once those thoughts were written, it was as if the pressure in her mind was eased.

What she had never found herself tempted to write was the positive things – oh, there might be a compliment here or there, for something exceptional, but, on the whole, the journal contained acid observations on the failings of the *ton* – their attitudes, manners, affairs and more. For the undesirable aspects of humanity were far more interesting to write about – and far more deserving of commentary, than the pleasant aspects. The pleasant aspects she treasured quietly in her thoughts, feeling no need to spill them onto the page.

What she was writing, this particular morning, was a discourse on the insipidity of the year's new crop of young women making their come outs. Lord Kevin's conversation, during the dance, where he had suggested that most common compliments were bland – and implied that so were most of their recipients – had inspired her to put down her thoughts on the matter. For they were bland – all of them.

Words like 'faded pastels' and 'conversation worthy of nothing more than ennui' seemed appropriate. Once she had finished a page of discussion of the failings of the hopeful young husband hunters, her thoughts turned to a far older generation. They fascinated her – the older dowagers and the chaperones, with their penchant for odd and extreme fashion choices, their outdated opinions on the world, and their apparent certainty that they deserved to be treated respectfully, no matter how badly they treated everyone else.

Amongst those women, there were definitely those worthy of being called a dragon, far more than Hyacinth was. Lady Dunwiddy for example – her attire the previous evening had been in a style twenty-five years out of date, in a virulent shade of puce, topped off by a turban with feathers.

So many feathers that Hyacinth had to wonder if her purchases had single-handedly required the activities of dozens of hunters, simply to collect them all. The effect was startling, and rather ludicrous. She was, any time that she walked close to a wall, at risk of the feathers brushing through the flames of the candles in the sconces – Hyacinth had watched, in horrified fascination, as she had nearly set herself alight multiple times.

Attempting to describe it all took more than a page, for there was just so much ridiculous detail to record. Like the multiple flounces on her gown, which made her look more like a child's overdecorated doll than anything else, and the less than subtle colour applied to her cheeks – she would have done well on the stage, with a face made up like that!

What Hyacinth wrote in that journal would never be seen by any eyes but her own – no matter how well it might suit the sort of scurrilous report that was found in gossip sheets like the 'Society Commentator', which was more commonly known amongst society as 'the Gossip Gazette' – just writing in it served her purpose adequately. The morning passed in a pleasant indulgence in sharp commentary, until Hyacinth felt relaxed, and relieved of the pressure that had been created by not saying it all to anyone at the Ball. Now, she could be as polite as necessary, no matter who called upon them today! Once she was done, she tucked the pencil between the pages of the journal, and returned it to its accustomed place in her drawer of assorted keepsakes – a drawer which the maids were forbidden to touch – and rang for Sally to come to help her dress.

As Sally did up the ridiculous number of little buttons on the back of her day dress, Hyacinth realised that it was still far earlier than she would normally have expected to be finished writing.

Why? Surely, there had been just as many people worthy of commentary at the previous evening's Ball as usual – so why had she written for less time?

And then it came to her. She felt a flush rise to her cheeks as she realised – she had written less, because she had noticed less – because she had been distracted, in a way that had never happened before.

She had been distracted by a man - Lord Kevin Loughbridge, that most unusual of gentlemen. A man she wanted to see again, and to dance with again.

Shocked at her own wishes, and at the intensity of that desire, Hyacinth pushed the thoughts away, and determinedly tried to turn her mind elsewhere. An effort at which she proved singularly inefficient.

CHAPTER THREE

The evening's event was obviously a crush, for the carriage spent a full twenty minutes inching forward in the queue, before their turn came to be set down before the imposing building. Hyacinth swallowed her impatience, and spent the time ignoring her sisters, and staring out the window, not really seeing what was before her. Would he be there? It was only a few days since she had met, and danced with, Lord Kevin Loughbridge, yet it seemed far longer.

The extent to which she desired his company annoyed her. She was not used to any man being able to influence her so much and, in fact, had always been sure that there was not a man in existence who could do so. It seemed that she had been wrong in that belief.

If he was there, would he dance with her again? And what might he say to her? For, of a certainty, there would be conversation worth having, if it was Lord Kevin to whom she spoke. A shiver ran through her at the thought – anticipation? Or apprehension? She was not sure.

By the time that they had finally made their way through the receiving line, and into the ballroom, that sensation had intensified, until it was almost unbearable. Hyacinth scanned the room, unable to help herself, looking for him. He wasn't there. A rush of disappointment ran through her, so intense that it left her reeling. She was still regaining her composure while Lily was greeted by Lord Canterford – who was, as always, unfailingly polite to all of them. For once, Hyacinth barely heard his words.

She had just managed to settle her senses and convinced herself that she really did not actually care all that much if Lord Kevin was not in attendance, when she had the odd sensation of being observed. Unable to help herself, she spun around, to find herself mere inches from those rich brown eyes, which regarded her with amusement.

Conflicting emotions filled her mind – annoyance, that he had startled her so, and that he most obviously knew it and was amused by it, delight, that he was there, and anger – that he was so easily able to discompose her completely. He winked at her, a most cheeky and impolite thing to do, and bowed - a perfect court bow, as if that wink had never happened.

"Lady Hyacinth, I trust that you are well? I have come, as you gave me permission to, to 'weather the storm' of your conversation once more. Might I claim a dance? Or would you prefer to walk on the terrace, or take a turn about the room?"

Hyacinth curtsied, suddenly breathless. He was teasing her! She flipped her fan across her face, the breeze welcome, for she could feel a flush heating her cheeks, and considered her words with care. Let him wait for her answer.

"You may claim a dance, Lord Kevin – although it seems that you will have to wait for some time, as the orchestra do not appear to be in place yet. But I will note your claim now, so that I do not forget, when I am deluged with attentive men, all seeking a space on my dance card."

Her tone was dry, the sarcasm obvious. Ostentatiously, she lifted the card, and wrote in his name.

He gave a soft laugh – a warm resonant sound that she felt on her skin, somehow – and bowed again.

"Perhaps then, whilst I endure the interminable wait, you might grant me a turn about the room? I am certain that your conversation will serve well to enliven the evening."

Enlivening... well that was a rather different description of her conversation than any she had heard before. She smiled, and when he offered his arm, she placed her hand upon it, and allowed him to lead her around the outskirts of the crowded room.

"And what, Lord Kevin, would you care to converse about? Do you find some topics more... enlivening... than others? Shall I hold forth on horticulture – a topic which everyone in our family has learnt in depth, as a consequence of our father's obsessions – or perhaps on fashion, as a young lady is expected to?"

His deep brown eyes laughed at her, but he appeared to give her questions true consideration, nonetheless.

"Horticulture... I had not considered. Perhaps another time, if the mood takes me. And fashion? You disappoint me, Lady Hyacinth – I had not expected so mundane a suggestion."

Hyacinth regarded him sidelong, her lips curving into a wry little smile. She would test him, test his resolve, test his ability to continue to enjoy her conversation. For part of her still struggled to believe that he actually wished to talk to her.

"Ah, but fashion can be discussed in multiple ways, Lord Kevin. There is the way that you were obviously thinking of, in which the latest new styles are discussed, and usually praised, with regard to those in the room who look their best on the evening of the conversation. That usually devolves into a conversation of mutual flattery and untruths between a group of ladies, all of whom are too scared to tell the others what they really think of their attire. And then there is the way that I find I prefer – a discussion which looks, unfalteringly, at the achievements in execrable taste which are on view in the room. For surely, some ladies must have put enormous effort into constructing an appearance which is so utterly unpleasant to view, and unflattering to their persons."

That warm laughter came again. Good, she had surprised him.

"Oh? Well, I must say, the latter does seem to provide far greater scope for amusing converse than the former. Do enlighten me – for I fear that, in general, I have ignored fashion – my own attire is usually on the plain side, and my sisters have excellent taste – but beyond that, I have never considered the detail – I either find something appealing, or I do not – and I admit that I often don't really notice much of it."

"How typical of a gentleman – of one who is not a fop, of course."

She looked around the room, choosing a suitable example.

He lifted his hand to his heart, making an affectation of being wounded by her words.

"Lady Hyacinth, are you implying that I am a... typical... gentleman? How lowering! And I had thought myself at least a little out of the ordinary – even if only in that I am most definitely not a fop!"

Hyacinth found herself laughing.

"I will, perhaps, grant that you are somewhat out of the ordinary, Lord Kevin. But there, I see an excellent example of the type of fashion worthy of note."

She indicated the far side of the room, where a cluster of older ladies stood in a corner, and watched Lord Kevin's face as he gazed in that direction. He made the oddest little sound, which she was almost certain was stifled laughter. She ignored it.

"I believe that I see the ladies you mean – but... which one, or ones, have received this accolade of 'worthy of discussion'?"

"Well, many of them would qualify, but I was noting one in particular. Lady Dunwiddy. She almost never disappoints – her attire is always chosen with what I can only describe as inspired skill – for how else could one make every single outfit that one chooses so utterly... painful... to the eye?"

It was definitely stifled laughter.

"Inspired skill? I see what you mean, I think – do you suggest that, with the scope of wardrobe that she undoubtedly owns, she is still completely incapable of putting together something pleasant and soothing to the eye?"

"Exactly. This evening's masterpiece is an excellent example. The orange with lime green lace is even more eye-catchingly inelegant than the puce which she wore to the last Ball. And the headdress... at least three peacocks must have been plucked of their entire tails to construct that! The pale blue net overlay on the skirt, with the badly beaded impressions of peacock feathers, is surely the crowning glory of this demonstration of sartorial bad taste. Every time I think that she cannot possibly outdo her previous performances, she does."

The laughter was no longer completely stifled. His eyes sparkled with amusement, far greater than she had seen before.

"Lady Hyacinth, you are truly a delight. But who do you normally converse with, on this topic of fashion in which I have discovered new interest?"

A shiver ran through her – what had she done? For she had just put into words things which should never be spoken, things which belonged only within the pages of her journal. If anyone of significance in society had overheard... but they had not, and Lord Kevin seemed not one whit displeased by what she had said. But she would need to be very careful when near him, in future – something about him made her forget herself.

"Why Lord Kevin, normally, I am my own listener, only, on such subjects. I discovered, a long time ago, that most of the *ton* do not share my... appreciation... for commentary on the finer proponents of... outrageous... fashion. I find them strangely unappreciative of a true assessment."

"Indeed, I can imagine that most ladies would not... cope... very well, with such crisp and unsparing review of their friends' fashion choices."

Hyacinth felt as if the world had gone mad. She could not, possibly, be having this conversation, with a man, at a Ball. She must be dreaming. Yet there he stood beside her, regarding her with warm laughing eyes, completely unconcerned with the sharpness of her words or her views on the world. The fact that he had not frowned, criticised, or simply abandoned her was rather intoxicating.

The orchestra struck up for the first set, and she felt a wash of relief. This conversation on fashion had gone quite far enough.

"I do believe that this is our dance, Lord Kevin."

He offered his arm.

"Then let us dance, by all means."

The dance passed in a blur, where they spoke less than before, each seeming a little caught up in their thoughts. It was a dance with very little time where the partners where in close contact, so conversation was more difficult. Yet Hyacinth was acutely aware of Lord Kevin, of every touch of his hand, and of his eyes following her, even when they did not speak. Once the music ended, and he escorted her back to her family, she found herself wishing for a way to keep him with her, longer.

But, as was polite and expected, he did not remain with her, but moved off into the room to speak to others he knew, after promising to see her again, and soon. The rest of the evening seemed dull after that, for everyone else that she spoke to was bland by comparison, and Hyacinth retreated into the habit of careful politeness. However, just when she thought that she might get through the evening without needing to dance with anyone else, she was jarred out of her reverie.

A gentleman who she had seen before, but never been introduced to, had approached her father. She had thought nothing of it – her father knew many gentlemen – until her father turned to her, and her sisters.

"Daughters, may I make known to you Abner Milne, Marquess of Puglinton. Puglinton, these are my daughters – Lady Lily, Lady Hyacinth, Lady Rose, Lady Camellia, Lady Primrose, Lady Violet and Lady Iris."

Lord Puglinton was an older man, a widower, if Hyacinth remembered correctly, and had not aged especially well. She suspected that he was not far past forty, yet he looked much older, with thinning hair and an expanding waistline which made his clothes seem ill-fitting. He looked at her, and her sisters, in a way that made her skin crawl. But he bowed politely to them all, and made some innocuous comment.

Hyacinth hoped that would be the last of it, but just as she expected him to turn away, politeness served, he stepped towards her, an almost predatory smile on his face.

"Lady Hyacinth, would you do me the honour of granting me a dance?"

There was only one dance remaining for the evening. She could not, in all politeness, refuse him. She was shocked – had he not heard of her reputation? Or had her dancing with Lord Kevin led Lord Puglinton to assume that perhaps that reputation was overstated? She swallowed, and nodded.

"Certainly, my Lord."

They were the very last words that she wanted to speak, but there was no choice, without making a scene.

She allowed him to lead her to the floor, her heart sinking as he did.

<<<< O >>>>

Kevin had found the rest of the evening, after that remarkable conversation with Lady Hyacinth, to be worthy of the ennui that he had pretended so often before. He wanted to go back to her, to talk to her more, to dance with her again - but he could not – not with the eyes of society upon them – that would be as good as a statement of intent. Which was a statement he did not wish to make. He did not know her well enough, yet, to consider such a thing.

But every conversation he had after hers was so bland as to induce sleep, and he found himself leaning against the wall, tucked away behind some potted palms, and simply watching her. He could not help himself – his eyes returned to her, no matter how often he made himself look away. The evening was drawing to a close, and he had not seen her dance with anyone else – were all of the men so blind as to not be able to see how intriguing she was? It seemed so. Perhaps he should simply leave, before the end of the evening.

As he went to move, a man approached her family. Kevin stopped again, watching. Puglinton, if he remembered the name aright. A widower rumoured to be looking for another wife. He watched the Duke perform introductions, and found his fists clenched when Puglinton took Lady Hyacinth's hand and bowed over it. Surely the man would move away, now that introductions were done. But he did not – instead, moments later, he led Lady Hyacinth to the floor, as the music began for the final dance of the evening.

Kevin forced himself to lean back against the wall, to adopt that so practiced pose of ennui, and watched. The man moved too close to Lady Hyacinth at every chance he got, and to Kevin it seemed that his hand held onto hers for a little longer than the dance required, every time they touched. He wanted to rush over there, and to shove Puglinton aside, to protect her from that overly familiar touch.

He forced himself to remain still. Of all women, Lady Hyacinth was well equipped to defend herself from unwanted attention - usually simply with very effective words. Yet his impulse to protect her was overwhelming. When the dance finally ended, and she had been returned to her family, he allowed himself to move. But he only departed once he had seen her family leave ahead of him.

Tomorrow, he would go to Chester Park – but the thought that Puglinton might dance with her again, whilst he was gone, was a nagging worry in his soul.

CHAPTER FOUR

"Wasn't Lord Puglinton simply disgusting?"

Primrose shuddered to emphasise her words. Hyacinth considered what to say – her other sisters were all watching her, waiting to see what she thought – all except Lily, who had not yet come down for the morning. In the end, she settled on the simplest answer.

"Yes, quite."

"Then why on earth did you dance with him, Hyacinth?"

Hyacinth sighed.

"Because, Primrose, I had no conceivable excuse not to – if I had refused him, it would have created a scene. And society already expects me to say outrageous things and create scenes. I do not need more of that – and neither do any of you. But yes, I found him rather repulsive. I wonder why Father introduced us? Lord Puglinton is not the usual sort of man to be an associate of our father."

"I introduced him for exactly the same reason that you danced with him – to avoid creating a socially unacceptable scene. The man had come to speak to me, and you were all right there – it would have been most unusual if I had not introduced you."

The girls spun to face their father, who had obviously overheard their conversation as he entered the parlour.

"Why do you think that he wanted to meet us?"

"Rumour suggests that he is looking for a wife. He is a widower – and you have dowries that might make any man look at you hopefully."

Hyacinth shuddered.

"You wouldn't even consider the idea – would you, Papa?"

The Duke sighed.

"No, I would not. I could see your reaction. You know that, no matter how much I hope for all of you to marry, I want you to be happy – I will never force a match upon you. But please, do try to find a man that you want to marry!"

At his words, Hyacinth found the image of Lord Kevin's face in her mind. It startled her – a man who she would want to marry? She pushed the idea away. She would marry one day, she was determined of it. But not yet.

"Thank you, Papa."

"Now, putting discussion of men that you do, and do not, like aside, I came to remind you that this evening is Lord Winstonholm's Ball, and ask you to be ready, early. Your mother is all of a dither about it."

"Of course. I am sure that we can manage that."

They spoke a little longer about the social events of the next few days, then the Duke left them to their conversation.

<<<< O >>>>

By late afternoon, the carriage was passing through peaceful countryside, where flowers abounded in the fields, and the warmth of spring had brought fresh growth everywhere. Kevin leant back against the squab of the carriage seat, idly watching the view. The opposite seat was piled with bundles, and small trunks – books for Maria, books for his father, and some small bolts of exquisite fabrics for his mother to have made up into whatever fashionable garment took her fancy.

He had told the coachman to take his time – they would overnight at a small Inn along the way, and reach Chester Park in the morning, all the better for not having rushed. Truth to tell, Kevin was a little unsure of his feelings – he wanted to see his family, but the worry about his father made him hesitant – almost as if, until he saw the evidence of whatever was wrong, he could pretend that no problem existed.

That was a fool's thinking, he knew, but nonetheless, his mind was turning that way. Part of him desperately wished to be back in London, rather than travelling steadily away from it. He had promised Lady Hyacinth that he would see her again, soon, and he intended to do so – but soon would not be before at least a week had elapsed. And that seemed, as the carriage took him further from her, as if it was a very long time indeed.

He laughed at his own thoughts, glad that no one shared his carriage to see it. When had he become so obsessed with the woman?

He did not know – but she excited him, captivated him, in a way that no other woman ever had. What might she think of his family? Or they of her? That thought popped into his mind, and he stopped, no longer noticing the world outside at all, as he considered it. Why would it matter what she thought? Yet it did. Disconcerted, he turned his mind away from it, leaving the idea for later consideration.

He leaned back again, and turned his eyes to the passing countryside, allowing the steady movement of the carriage to lull him towards sleep. When it came, it came with dreams - of soft caramel hair and intense blue eyes.

<<<< O >>>>

The Winstonholm Ball was crowded, and Hyacinth was swept along with her sisters, into the tangle of people they knew. As usual, the attention of gentlemen was all for the other girls, not Hyacinth. Hopefully, Hyacinth's eyes roamed the room, but did not find the one man they sought. Lord Kevin was not present.

She chided herself for a fool, so deep was her disappointment – but she kept looking. He had promised to see her again, soon, after all. As her sisters were swept away to dance, and she faced another evening of being avoided by those who feared the dragon, she carefully assumed her 'social mask', and settled to observing the attendees, allowing that part of her mind which would document it all later, in her journal, to gather the information it needed.

Amongst the younger women, the evening's gowns seemed to indicate a new trend, of overdone flounces around the bodice, decorated with small tangles of ribbon.

It was not flattering, on the vast majority of the girls who wore it. As Hyacinth watched them, fascinated as always by the fact that someone had convinced them to wear such things, when they were manifestly not suited to the wearer, a clearing of the throat disturbed her concentration. She turned, annoyed.

Lord Puglinton stood before her, smiling a rather false looking smile. Her skin crawled as his eyes traversed her body, then returned to meet her gaze.

"Lady Hyacinth – you seem distracted – did you not hear me speak?"

"No, my Lord, I fear that I was woolgathering. There are so many exemplars of the latest fashions at an event like this, it is very easy to become distracted."

It was an answer which she had used before, when asked what on earth she was looking at / thinking about. The words were all that was expected of a lady, if one interpreted them as most men did. But they were also true – it was just that Hyacinth's perspective on them was quite the opposite of what others expected it to be. Lord Puglinton made the usual assumptions.

"Women seem to think of nothing else but fashion. Still, if that amuses you..."

"It does, my Lord, far more than you might think."

"Good, good. Now, Lady Hyacinth, will you grant me the next dance?"

Hyacinth stilled for a moment. She could not escape it. It was blatantly obvious that she was not ill, or incapacitated in any way, and there were no other gentlemen waiting.

She inclined her head, and placed her hand on his proffered arm. He led her to the floor, and she forced herself to ignore the whispers around her. The same people who spoke of her shrewishness were now waiting to see what would happen – would Lord Puglinton be delivered a set down from her sharp tongue, enough to make him abandon her? She suspected that they all hoped for such a thing, for a moment of delicious scandal to brighten their evening.

She would give them no such thing. She might apply the sharpness of her tongue, but she would not, for her sisters' sake, allow it to create scandal.

The dance, this time, left them face to face for much of it. Lord Puglinton chose to converse.

"Lady Hyacinth, if I may say so, I am somewhat startled by the fact that you were not surrounded by gentleman admirers, when I approached you this evening. Can it be that something dissuades them?"

Hyacinth clenched her teeth for a moment. The man was beyond impolite!

"Why my Lord, I believe that you have the right of it. For it has come to my attention that I am rumoured to be rather a shrew. Surely you have heard these rumours? I cannot imagine that a man as well connected as you seem to be would be uninformed on such matters."

He blinked at her, as they turned about one another in the slow wheel of the dance. So, he had heard, but had not truly believed what he had been told. She clenched her teeth again, this time to prevent herself from laughing.

"And does that not worry you, my Lady? Surely the life of a spinster does not appeal to you, and you are rather... well..."

Did his rudeness never end? Hyacinth smiled as sweetly as she could manage, remembering Lord Kevin's words about a vixen's sharp teeth and cunning, and ability to hide in plain sight.

"Does it worry me that some might call me a spinster now? No, my Lord, it does not. I will marry when I am ready."

The slight widening of his eyes indicated that he had not expected that answer.

"I see – how very... unusual... of you. I would have thought that your father would have something to say on the matter. In fact, I am somewhat surprised that he has not yet simply arranged a match for you. After all, your dowry is... substantial, and your figure is not... unappealing. A gentleman could most certainly overlook your unfortunate... manner... in the light of those things."

Hyacinth breathed deeply, forcing herself to remain calm. The man was beyond insulting, and yet seemed to think that he had said nothing out of place.

"I am sure that many a gentleman could, my Lord. But you make the assumption that I would accept an offer from such a man. I do not feel the pressure to marry so keenly that I would do such a thing."

"And your father allows you this rebellious attitude? I wonder how long that will last, as you grow older."

"I do not know, my Lord, but I am quite certain that I will find out."

Hyacinth smiled at him sweetly, wishing nothing more than to spit in his face, as she had been told camels did to men they disliked. He gave her the oddest look, as if he knew something that she did not. Then, blessedly, the music ended. He held to her hand for far longer than was appropriate, as they came to a halt. She tugged it away from his grasp, and he smiled – a most unpleasant smile.

He led her back to her family, and she wondered how she would bear it, if he intended to ask her to dance at every Ball – for she would attend every Ball, regardless, if for no other reason than that she might see Lord Kevin there. She clung to that thought, feeling acutely the lack of Lord Kevin's presence, for the conversation with Lord Puglinton had made it intensely clear to her why she found Lord Kevin's conversation so intriguing. Lord Kevin treated her as a person, entitled to their own opinions. Lord Puglinton, like so many other men, apparently saw her as a possession, to be traded between men for their own purposes, and her dowry as her most attractive attribute.

Her sisters looked at her with sympathy once Lord Puglinton had walked away, and she allowed herself to relax a little. Primrose came to her, and actually patted her hand consolingly – truly, Hyacinth's control must be slipping, if her sister could see the extent of her distress!

Somehow, she endured the rest of the evening, forcing herself to observe others, and, most inappropriately, to imagine delivering her commentary on them to Lord Kevin, rather than simply writing it in her journal. Imagining that helped, even if she could never actually allow herself to do so again.

Chester Park was exceptionally beautiful in the springtime, and Kevin felt himself somehow better there, after the soot of London. Maria was much improved in attitude, and he felt sure that Charles would propose to her very soon. As a result, both Lord and Lady Chester were happier than they had been for more than a year.

The gifts that Kevin had brought were gratefully received, and, overall, they made the picture of a happy family. But Kevin's father still seemed, somehow, not quite right. He was quieter, and spent more time in his study, or the library, rather than out and about on the estate. He seemed thinner – not a lot, but enough for Kevin to notice – and his face held a pallor, where previously he had tended towards ruddy cheeks. Perhaps it was just that he was spending more time indoors.

Even as he thought that, Kevin knew, instinctively, that it was not true. There was something wrong. Late that first night, when his mother and sister had retired to bed, he sat in the study with his father, sipping a brandy. He had to try, had to ask, somehow, and hope that his father would tell him what was amiss.

"It looks to me as if you have been slaving away over the estate books far more than ever before, Father. What has provoked this industriousness? Is there something that concerns you?"

Lord Chester lifted his gaze from his brandy, and considered his son for a moment, as if weighing what to say. Then he gave the tiniest shake of his head, and his expression shifted to a somewhat brittle smile. Kevin knew, in that instant, that the words he would hear would not reveal anything to him.

"There are no problems with the estates – have no fear on that account – but I have found myself motivated to pay more attention. If I am to have Charles Barrington as a son-in-law, it behoves me to do at least as well with my estates as he has done for Melton. When the time comes, I'll not be handing you a tangle of problems, I promise you."

"May that time be long in coming."

For a moment, Lord Chester stilled, and Kevin saw a tiny spasm pass through him, as if he forcibly prevented himself from coughing, or speaking. Then he lifted his brandy to his lips, and Kevin wondered if he had imagined it. But he did not think he had.

"A worthy wish. But I don't dwell on such things. They happen in God's own time, regardless of what we mortals desire. Enough of such maudlin thinking – tell me of what is happening in town – who is the toast of the Season, and what foolishness do young men believe is dashing this year?"

Kevin obliged, and recounted what he could of people his father knew, and of the idiosyncrasies of the *ton* in general. Doing so made him think, again, of Lady Hyacinth, and her most astringent commentary on sartorial bad taste. Even in the face of his father's unwillingness to speak of whatever troubled him, the thought of Lady Hyacinth brought a smile to Kevin's face.

CHAPTER FIVE

A week had passed since Hyacinth had last seen Lord Kevin, and it felt like an eternity. She was irritable – annoyed with herself for being so obsessed with a man – for that was behaviour that she had always despised when she saw it in others – and here she was, doing that herself, even whilst she teased Lily about being smitten with Lord Canterford!

Truly, she should not tease her sister so, for she had become almost certain that Lord Canterford would offer for Lily soon. And that Lily would be happy with that. To see her sister pleased by a man was remarkable, and reassuring – she would not want Lily to spend her life a spinster, any more than she wished to do so herself.

Hyacinth stood in the parlour, staring out the window at the fenced park in the middle of the square. At this time of year, it was delightful, and she intended to slip out to sit there with her journal one morning soon. It was a risk to take the journal out of the house, but the spring garden called to her, after the long months of winter cold.

As she stood there dreaming, she saw, through the greenery, the front of a house on the farthest side of the square from their own. It had been vacant for some time, and she had supposed that whoever owned it had retired to the country, or perhaps had chosen not to let it for the Season. But, as she watched the door opened, and a gentleman came out. Hyacinth sucked in her breath, barely preventing herself from gasping aloud.

For the gentleman exiting the house was none other than Lord Puglinton! If he had taken the house for the Season, then it would be almost impossible to avoid seeing him at times – and he might choose to call upon them, now that he was a close neighbour. The thought horrified her. But she would not let that stop her from spending time in the park. Surely, he would not be inclined to wander in the park – most gentlemen didn't.

He walked off down the street, and Hyacinth turned back to the room, where her sisters were discussing the merits of various foods – a conversation undoubtedly started by Rose, who was, at that moment, lamenting the fact that foods went stale, or rotten, so fast, when she often would have liked to save some of a particular cake or dish for days later. The others laughed at her earnestness on the topic, yet could not help but agree to some extent.

The day passed in a pleasant enough manner, but Hyacinth found her thoughts turning back to that glimpse of Lord Puglinton, and from there to the times during this last week that he had danced with her. No matter how blunt she was in her comments to the man, or how much she expressed her most unladylike opinions, he did not desist. He had even implied, the previous evening, that he would actually offer for her.

It made her feel ill. She was so very glad that Papa would never agree unless she did, no matter what Lord Puglinton might expect.

She steeled herself for the evening – which was to be a Ball at the Earl of Porthaven's home – and prayed that Lord Kevin would be there – not that he could save her from being trapped into dancing with Lord Puglinton again, but at least, if he was there, she might dance with him also, might converse with someone who seemed to actually appreciate her conversation, rather than condemning her for it.

<<<< O >>>>

The London air, even scented by the spring flowers which filled the gardens of the aristocracy, still had a sooty undertone to it which Kevin was acutely aware of after the week spent at Chester Park. As the carriage set him down before Porthaven House, his heart beat faster – surely, she would be there. It seemed forever since he had seen Lady Hyacinth, since he had heard her delightfully sharp assessment of the world around her, and he almost rushed up the stairs in his need to see her.

But he forced himself to slow, to adopt that stylish, casual air of ennui. He would not make a fool of himself. In the ballroom, the crowds of hopeful young women fluttered about, as always – a sea of white and pale pastel gowns, overburdened with flounces and lace, with here and there the startling contrast of a stronger colour, usually worn by a far older woman, or by a gentleman of fashion. Kevin scanned the room, almost desperate to find her – and aware of how foolish that desperation was. He repressed a desire to laugh at his own behaviour.

As he moved further into the room, he was still looking. Then, unexpectedly, a path cleared through the crowd in front of him, and he saw her. At that instant, she looked up, and their eyes met. It was as if the rest of the room faded away. Dimly, he was aware that he had stopped – suddenly enough that someone had almost collided with him. Their muttered 'really!' as they narrowly avoided him brought him back to his senses. He began to move again, and the crowd closed between them.

By the time he reached where she still stood, he had calmed his racing heart a little, but the sight of her took his breath away. She was more beautiful than ever, and her smile was more than welcoming. As he bowed over her hand, she flushed a little, and he hoped that was a sign that she was as happy to see him as he was to see her.

"Lady Hyacinth. You look charming, as always. Might we take a turn about the room? And might I hope for a dance?"

"Lord Kevin. Yes, I would be happy to grant you both."

As she spoke, her eyes flicked past him, and narrowed for a moment. He wondered why. Saying nothing more, he offered her his arm, and led her away towards the edge of the room. Her sigh of relief was quite audible to him.

"Lady Hyacinth, what brings you to sigh so?"

Her eyes turned to his, and she hesitated a moment before speaking.

"Relief. You have just saved me from a moment that I was dreading. Your timing is impeccable."

"Oh? And exactly what is it, that I have saved you from?"

"Lord Puglinton."

Kevin glanced back the way that they had come. Lord Puglinton stood, not far from Lady Hyacinth's family, glaring after them. The man was, most obviously, not happy.

"I see. I gather that Lord Puglinton has found it in himself to overcome the fear of your dragonish reputation – and that you are displeased with that fact?"

"That is a fair summary of the situation, yes. The man is rude, and arrogant beyond belief. His conversation ranges from the offensive to the sublimely ridiculous, and his unpleasant manner is only exceeded by his poor taste in waistcoats. He seems to think that I am a despairing spinster, who would marry anything that offered for her. And nothing that I say dissuades him from pursuing me – I believe that he hopes that father will direct me to marry him, should he offer for me. It is as if he is deaf and blind to reality – or perhaps he needs money so badly that my dowry blinds him to all else."

"When described that way, he sounds quite the most obnoxious man I have ever heard of. Yet as to your assessment of his potential desire for your dowry... I seem to remember hearing that he has substantial investments, in all sorts of businesses – so I do not know that he needs money to the degree you suggest."

Her eyes met his – she seemed startled by this insight.

"Then why on earth does he pursue me, and completely ignore everything that I say to him?"

"I cannot answer that for a certainty, but... forgive me for my rather inappropriate implication... but I suspect that what blinds him is not your dowry, but your other... assets... which it would be hard for him to fail to notice."

She lowered her eyes from his for a moment, and he worried that he had offended her with his indelicate words, but then she raised her chin, and looked at him, a wry smile twisting her lips.

"Oh dear! How unfortunate – do you really believe him to be so taken with my bosom, and my physical... potential... that he can truly ignore every word that I say, and believe that he could do so for the rest of his life?"

Kevin felt the smile on his own face widen – she was delightful – so refreshingly honest and open. With any other woman, he might never have risked such words, and if he had, would expect to have been spurned for his rudeness – yet here she was, as amused as he by the shallowness of men like Lord Puglinton.

"I do believe exactly that. You noted, yourself, his arrogance – I am sure that he rarely truly hears what others say to him, for he is too busy valuing himself."

"I begin to see how it might be that his first wife became ill, and eventually died – a man like that would be beyond wearing on the soul!"

"Indeed. Can you not avoid him?"

"And pray how might I do that? He has done nothing outwardly inappropriate, and I cannot simply refuse to dance with him, when I dance with others, and am obviously in robust health. And I will not feign illness, for then, how might I dance or walk with you?"

Kevin's breath hitched – had she just implied? She had. A spiral of ridiculous happiness curled through him. Her bluntness was wonderful, and she was so open with him.

He had, in that moment, an intense desire to kiss her. He forced his mind away from that thought, and back to their conversation.

"I am honoured, my Lady. But if you continue to dance with him, will he not assume that his suit might be welcome? If he actually spoke to your father..."

"He can assume all he wishes, and he can speak to my father, but it will gain him nothing. My father will not force me to a match, no matter how desperately he, and my mother, wish that I might marry. That fact is the only thing that allows me to persist with being minimally polite to the man. That, and the hope of conversation with you, to balance the scales. With you, I can speak of things that others in society would most certainly regard as inappropriate conversation!"

"You can, and I value the fact that you trust me enough to do so."

"I am not quite certain, Lord Kevin, how that came to be the case – but I also value it, greatly."

They walked a little further, drifting into a companionable silence, as she observed the people in the room, and he observed her doing so. When they reached that end of the room, the orchestra struck up for the next set, and he bowed to her again, before leading her on to the floor. This time, it was a waltz, and his heart thundered in his chest as he took her into his arms. She smiled up at him, and the desire to kiss her rushed through him again. He licked his lips, resisting the urge. Conversation seemed the safest option.

"So, my Lady, what are your observations on this evening's fashion?"

Those soft blue eyes met his, suddenly sparkling with mischief.

"Why Lord Kevin, I thought that you had declared yourself uninterested in fashion? But, as you ask... tonight, I have been observing the sartorial achievements of the gentlemen. I believe that Lord Middenhall has managed the greatest achievement in fashionable ostentation this evening. His combination of red and blue pinstripes on his waistcoat, with a mustardy gold coat and maroon paisley breeches is obviously a work of art in its own right. Rarely have I struggled so not to flinch when greeted by a gentleman."

Her tone was so delicately sarcastic that he laughed, delighted again. And her assessment was quite accurate. As they had walked around the room, he had, even though very focussed on the woman at his side, been unable to avoid noting Lord Middenhall, for that mustard coloured coat was remarkably bright.

"A fine and accurate assessment, my Lady, I must agree with you. But tell me – do you develop opinions upon other aspects of those around us, apart from fashion? What of the gossip, and the poorly hidden affairs and scandals – do they attract your discerning eye?"

She actually blushed, and bit her lip a little – it made him want to kiss her even more. Then her eyes met his, full of challenge.

"Do you imply, my Lord, that a gently reared lady such as I would know anything at all of scandalous liaisons, of the sort that the gossips whisper about?"

They swirled around, the dance effortless.

With her, he need not think - somehow, the dancing just happened. He smiled, deeply amused.

"My Lady, I do not imply anything. But the fact that I have sisters leads me to believe that gently reared young ladies know far more of the scandalous goings on of society than they ever admit to. And your keenly observant eye would surely notice the tiny things that betray those attempting to keep secrets…"

She laughed – the sound ran through him, like a rush of heat.

"Perhaps you are correct, my Lord, although I, of course, will not admit to any such thing. But I will direct your attention to Lady Gosham, whose elderly husband is rarely seen out in society, and Lord Bessmark, who seems to be always quite close to her…"

Kevin glanced about the room, as the dance rotated them, eventually discovering the couple Lady Hyacinth had mentioned. They were tucked away in an alcove, almost screened from view by potted palms. They sat very close together, and Lord Bessmark's hand appeared to be behind Lady Gosham. He gave a quiet snort of laughter, and Lady Hyacinth's smile widened.

So, she observed that sort of thing too. Oh, how he wished that he could speak to her in true privacy, and hear the unexpurgated version of her thoughts on the affairs of society. It would be, he was quite certain, far more accurate than the gossip sheets. The music slowed, and he realised, with a start, that the dance was about to end.

She looked up at him, and whispered, her voice so soft that he could barely make out the words.

"When you return me to my family, I pray, do not abandon me. Stay, and speak to my father, or my sisters, as well as to me – anything will do as a topic, but allow me to hope that your presence may deter Lord Puglinton."

"Of course, my Lady."

It seemed to work – Puglinton glared, but did not approach, and Kevin spent the rest of the evening discussing agriculture with the Duke of Elbury, who, although far more interested in flowers, was a positive font of knowledge on the topic of modern methods of farming. It was a surprisingly pleasant conversation. Lady Hyacinth looked at him with gratitude, and his heart sang in response.

<<<< O >>>>

After the Ball at Porthaven House, where Lord Kevin's presence had deterred Lord Puglinton, Hyacinth had been hopeful that the man would abandon his pursuit of her. She had been disappointed in that hope.

The next three Balls, whilst she danced and spoke with Lord Kevin, that no longer prevented Lord Puglinton from asking her to dance. She had done the socially correct thing, and agreed, hating every moment of it. But she had been cheered by the fact that Lord Kevin watched her. Somehow, his eyes upon her had made her feel safer.

Until tonight – when he was not in attendance. She felt bereft without his presence, and Lord Puglinton's leering smile did nothing to ease her dismay.

CHAPTER SIX

The sisters sat in the parlour, chattering away about a random collection of things – men, fashion, dogs, horses, painting, books and more. Hyacinth was, as always, amused by her sisters' vastly differing views of the world. But today, when Hyacinth most wanted to not think about the previous evening, and the ways of society, her sisters kept coming back to a discussion of gentlemen. And, in addition to that, Lily seemed distracted – far more than usual, and had barely said a word.

Hyacinth turned to her.

"What do you think Lily? Should Rose allow a gentleman's opinions on food to influence her view of him? It seems rather shallow to me."

Lily blinked at Hyacinth a moment, then, as Hyacinth waited, shook herself out of her woolgathering to answer.

"If it matters to Rose, why should she not let it influence her view of him? Surely, we should each choose who to like, based on what matters to us."

"I see – so, do tell us, what is it about Lord Canterford's likes or dislikes that matters to you, Lily? Or are you still trying to pretend that you are not smitten, even though he calls on you almost every second day?"

Lily blinked and Hyacinth wondered what was wrong with her – certainly Lily did not always like being teased, but usually managed to take it in good part – but her expression said that today, she was not at all happy.

"Oh Hyacinth, stop it! Cannot you leave me alone on the matter? Yes, I do like him, if you must hear the words from my mouth! But I cannot answer your question, for I fear that this last few weeks I have become less and less sure of what he cares about, what matters in his life. It is all so frustrating, and quite lowering. I thought that he cared for me, but now…"

Her voice tailed off, and Hyacinth looked at her, a little shocked. The other sisters' conversations stopped, and they all turned to look at Lily. Lily never snapped, not even when teased unmercifully. Something was obviously wrong. Camellia came to sit beside Lily, and took her hand.

"What do you mean, Lily? What are you unsure of?"

A strangled sob escaped Lily, and slow tears trickled down her cheeks. Rose produced a handkerchief, only slightly discoloured by icing from the cakes they had just had with tea, and handed it to her silently. Lily gulped.

"I… I thought that he cared, yet whilst we talk, and I enjoy his company, and he seems to enjoy mine, there has been nothing further. Not since… not since one moment, weeks ago. Since then, he has not attempted to hold my hand, to be closer than propriety dictates, or to kiss me, or… anything! It is as if I am a sister to him, not someone he might… he might marry!"

"Do you want him to marry you, Lily?"

Camellia's words dropped into a pool of silence. The ripple of thought that they created spread through the room, and six sets of eyes studied Lily's face, waiting for her answer. Lily drew a long breath, and Hyacinth felt as if something momentous was about to be said.

"Yes, I believe that I do want him to marry me. But I have obviously been a fool – I have been seduced by the comfort of our conversation, into allowing him to see far too much of my intellectual habits. Surely that is why he has become so distant from me – no matter what he says, surely he is like every other man of the *ton*, and does not really want too much intelligence in his wife. After all, an intelligent wife might argue with him, might dare to have her own opinion."

There was bitter sadness in Lily's voice and Hyacinth found herself achingly in sympathy with her sister. She was personally all too aware of the attitude of most gentlemen of the *ton*, to a woman who dared to have opinions, and express them. But she had concluded, at least a year ago, that a man who would not hear a woman's opinion was not worth spending time on – and Lily needed to recognise that too. Hyacinth snorted.

"If that is true of him, then you are better without him. But I can't believe it."

"You can't?"

"I can't. The man is far sharper than he allows most people to notice, and far more respectful of women's opinions than almost any man I have met – with the obvious exception of our father, and a few others. I think that you are letting your fears run away with you."

"Oh Hyacinth, I so want you to be right!"

Camellia squeezed Lily's hand, and Lily turned to meet her eyes.

"Lily, you know that not all men prefer their wives dull and uneducated -- look at the people we know – the Duchess of Melton designs gardens, the Countess of Porthaven runs an art gallery – yet they are loved by men who appreciate their skills and interests. Compared to that, my dear Lily, you are almost ordinary – so why should you not be loved? Do not let yourself lose the only man I have ever seen you care for at all, just because you fear that he does not appreciate the real you. Surely, there is some other reason for his reticence of late. Why do you not simply ask him if anything is amiss. You could, perhaps, even be brave, and declare your feelings, and see what happens."

Lily looked at Camellia, blinking as if somewhat stunned by the words. Hyacinth considered them too. Camellia had a way of going to the heart of things, in the kindest possible manner. Finally, Lily spoke again.

"You are right, Camellia, I need to know the truth, not torture myself with imagined reasons for his manner. But the idea of declaring myself to him, of risking rejection – that is quite terrifying."

Hyacinth considered Lily's statement. She realised, in that moment, that she liked Lord Kevin – rather more than she had ever liked a gentleman before – and that the idea of telling him that was, as Lily had called it, quite terrifying. How would she feel, if she were in the situation that Lily was in now? She suspected that she would be just as uncertain.

"I believe that I agree Camellia. If... if I ever start to think like Lily has been thinking, please shake me hard, and tell me what you just told Lily."

Lily gave Hyacinth a hard look, obviously startled by what she had said, and Hyacinth swallowed – had Lily realised, even though she had been so distracted lately by Lord Canterford, that Hyacinth was coming to care for Lord Kevin? Then Lily dropped her eyes from Hyacinth's, and spoke.

"Thank you, all of you. You have made me determined. When he next calls, I will ask him about his reticence, and, perhaps, if I can gather up the courage, even tell him of my feelings – for knowing the truth of it would be far better than this perpetual uncertainty."

The sisters applauded, and Lily seemed cheered by their support. Rose pushed a fresh cup of tea into Lily's hand, and placed a plate of cakes beside her. In Rose's world, tea and cakes could fix anything, as they all knew.

They went back to speaking of ordinary things, and Lily joined the conversation normally, but Hyacinth found herself still distracted by the questions that Lily's distress had triggered in her thoughts. Just how much did she care for Lord Kevin? And... why had he not been at the Ball the previous evening? After the last week or so, when he had spoken with her, danced with her, at every event, his sudden unexplained absence disturbed her.

It was like the previous time – one day he was there, the next he was gone, for a week or more, with no warning, and no explanation. What could possibly take him from London like that, especially if he truly did wish to spend time with Hyacinth?

She did not know, but it did not seem the actions of a man who might truly care for her. Perhaps, dreadful thought, he had a mistress somewhere, tucked away in a pretty country cottage, and that was where he disappeared to. She did not wish to believe such a thing of him, but she was not an innocent fool – men had mistresses, and men happily courted young ladies, whilst still enjoying those mistresses.

She stilled, all awareness of the rest of the room fading away. 'Courting' – was that what had been happening between them, however informally? It might, she realised, be perceived that way. Had anyone noticed? Probably. Did she care? That they noticed – no, she cared nothing for that – she was watched regardless, what was one more aspect to that? But... did she want it to be courtship?

That was a far harder question to answer.

<<<< O >>>>

The following morning, after yet another Ball where Lord Kevin was not present, but Lord Puglinton was, Hyacinth sat abed with her journal on her lap, pouring her frustrations with the situation onto the page, in the form of particularly acid commentary on the previous evening. She had intended to take her journal to the park that day, but had woken to the sound of a steady light rain. So she curled in her bed, with a cup of rich heated chocolate beside her.

Once the writing had eased the pressure in her mind, and she had space to think of other things beyond the scandals of the *ton*, and their dreadful fashion sense, her thoughts turned back to the previous day's conversation with her sisters.

She had still not answered her own question.

Did she want it to be courtship?

She began to suspect that she did. At that thought, fear filled her. It seemed that, for now, he found her sharp tongue and acid observations amusing – but how long could that last? Surely, like most men, he would come to find it wearing, would come to resent the fact that she disturbed his peace of mind, by having such outspoken opinions. And what would happen then? If he had a mistress, if that was where he went, when he suddenly disappeared from London for days, then surely, when he tired of Hyacinth's sharp tongue, he would go to that mistress. That was not the sort of marriage she wanted.

She lifted her chocolate and sipped, torn between the desire to laugh and to cry. Here she was, building castles out of air, imagining that a man who had shown her interest and courtesy – truthfully, the first man to ever really do so – was not only courting her, but would marry her. It was absurd. But having thought it all, she could not so simply erase it from her mind. Somehow, she had to be patient, to discover whether he did, in truth have a mistress, and whether he actually cared for her at all, beyond finding her an option for light entertainment at Balls.

Discovering that, of course, was dependent upon him reappearing in London – something which she could not guarantee would happen, no matter how much she might wish it.

<<<< O >>>>

When he arrived at Chester Park, Kevin found himself swept up in a whirl of happiness. Charles had, it seemed, finally asked Maria to marry him, and been accepted. They had all expected this, but to have it confirmed was wonderful.

Maria was nervous, yet gaining in confidence about venturing back into society, to some degree, and his mother was delighted – she had another wedding to plan. His father was equally happy, for he had always liked Charles, and respected Charles astute management of his brother's estates, but in that happiness, Kevin detected something more – almost a sense of relief, as if seeing Maria settled and happy sooner rather than later was of the utmost importance.

It wore at him, that little inconsistency, that inexplicable element to his father's attitude, and he determined to spend time with his father, again, to try to get him to admit to whatever was amiss with him. For Kevin was more certain than ever that something was.

On the last evening before his planned departure from Chester Park, he found himself, again, sitting with his father in the study, brandy in hand, after everyone else had gone to bed.

"Are you happy, Father, that Maria will marry again?"

"I am, I am. Wareham is a good man, and genuinely loves her, as she loves him. After that fiasco of a first marriage for her, I would have done anything to see her happy. And now I will – I already do, for she positively lights up when in his presence."

Kevin sipped his brandy, carefully assessing his father's words. The way that Lord Chester had said 'and now I will' was odd, as if he had not expected to do so. Yet he was not an old man – he was in his fifties, what should be the prime of his life for a man who had always had a good life.

"That is good to hear – but tell me – did you ever truly doubt that she would find happiness? I could not imagine her hiding away in sadness forever."

His father's eyes brightened, almost as if he held back tears, and Kevin blinked – surely it was an effect of the flickering light from the fire, an illusion?

"Oh, I was sure that she would overcome the past, eventually. But I was not sure how long that might take..."

Kevin nodded. There it was again, that unspoken implication that his father might not have all the time in the world. The worry settled deeper into his bones. He decided to take a risk.

"Father, forgive me for asking, but is something amiss with you? You seem, somehow, more... worried?... about the future than you used to be. Does something trouble you?"

Lord Chester met his son's eyes, which were so like his own, and hesitated. Kevin waited, hoping that his father might reveal what it was that worried him. After a moment, Lord Chester looked away, and lifted his brandy with a slight shake of his head. There was a moment, a small sound, a small movement – as before, like a stifled cough, then he sipped the rich brown liquid, before meeting Kevin's eyes again.

"No, no, nothing is amiss. I just like things to be in order. The older I get, the more that seems to matter to me. But on that note, tell me – have you not yet found a woman who appeals to you? I would see all my children married and happy..."

Kevin was startled – his father had never pressed him on the matter of marriage before, even though he was an only son, and knew that it was his duty to marry and get himself an heir. Something was definitely odd with his father, there was no doubt at all. The man was far too stubborn to admit it, it seemed.

But his words had brought to Kevin's mind an image of Lady Hyacinth, which startled him even more. Was he truly beginning to consider Lady Hyacinth in that light? As a potential bride? Two months earlier, he would have laughed at the very idea – now, it did not seem so preposterous.

"Not yet Father. I will be sure to inform you, as soon as I do."

"Good, good, and do make it soon."

They spoke a little longer, about the planning for Maria's wedding, then Kevin took himself off to bed. But the thoughts of Lady Hyacinth stayed with him. How did he truly feel about her? If he was honest with himself, he knew that she meant more to him than simply amusing conversation at social events – but what did she feel for him? She was always so self-contained, so confident and perceptive, yet she showed little of her feeling to others. He did not know, at all, what she really thought of him.

And he wanted to, with a sudden urgency. He resolved that, upon his return to London, he would call upon her, would allow himself to go further than just conversation at Balls, at least until he discovered whether she was at all interested in anything more.

He certainly hoped that she was. The sight of Charles and Maria's happiness had made him, just a little, jealous.

CHAPTER SEVEN

The sun was warm on Hyacinth's face as she walked across the square and into the fenced park. She wound through the flower bordered paths until she came to the bench she preferred — set among trees and bushes as part of an artfully constructed folly, with a tangle of ivy and other plants all about it, almost underfoot.

It was early, by the standards of the *ton*, and almost completely quiet. Birds twittered in the trees, and there was, in the distance, the ever-present rumble of carriage wheels on cobbles, but otherwise no sound distracted her.

She settled onto the bench with a sigh of pleasure, and drew her journal and pencil from the pockets of her simple day dress. The previous evening had been another horrible one — oh, not that anything truly bad had happened, but Lord Kevin had not been there, and Lord Puglinton had — again. The man's conversation became worse every time that she danced with him, and his insinuations that, should he offer for her, she might be forced to wed him, had become more blatant.

Her writing that morning was therefore rather influenced by the experience, and had become a treatise on the arrogance of gentlemen who thought themselves to be a desirable match, with side comments on the degree to which they usually lacked elegance as well as sense. It was, as always, a relief to write and to allow her thoughts free rein after the effort that it had taken the night before, not to outright insult the man. She still valued her sisters' reputations, if not her own, and had bitten her tongue, so hard had it been to stay silent, and seem unaware of the insult that he did her with almost every word that he spoke.

Soon, as the process of writing took her, her awareness of other things faded away, and the peace of the location drew the tension out of her. By the time that she was almost ready to stop writing, the sun had risen near to its highest point, and the square was waking up around her. She was vaguely aware of the sound of a carriage nearby, but ignored it, concentrating on the last sentence of the description that she wrote.

"Lady Hyacinth?"

The voice came from very close by, just the other side of the row of thick bushes. She hastily slipped the pencil between the pages of the journal, and shoved it under her skirts, feeling her way to getting it into her pocket. She was just in time – as her hands closed together in her lap, Tomps, one of the footmen from Elbury House, came around the bushes

"Yes Tomps?"

"My Lady, your mother sent me to find you. You have a gentleman caller."

"A caller? Who is it?"

Her heart beat harder, and her breath, already short from the shock of nearly being discovered writing in her journal, became even more rushed. Tomps held out a card. She rose, and took it, feeling the tug as her journal slipped into her pocket further.

'Lord Kevin Loughbridge'

The crisp black text on the unadorned card declared his presence. He had come to call on her! Her heart lifted, full of joy, even as she cautioned herself not to be a fool – she had not seen him for more than a week, and she had no idea where he had been – all of her doubts came rushing back. But they did nothing to reduce her eagerness to see him.

As she followed Tomps back to the house, she considered her appearance – which was most certainly not suitable for receiving callers! They stepped into the entryway, and she turned to the footman.

"Please, ensure that Lord Kevin is served tea, and assure him that I will be there very soon – but I simply must change first."

He nodded, and she almost ran up the stairs, nearly colliding with Sally as she reached her bedroom door.

"Quickly Sally, I must change, into a dress suitable for receiving callers!"

The maid ran into the dressing room, and returned with an appropriate gown, as Hyacinth undid the loose and unfashionable day dress she wore, and let it drop onto her bed. Within minutes, she was buttoned into the other gown, and her hair had been pinned up into an elegant knot.

Sally turned towards the discarded gown.

"Leave it, please, I will deal with it later – I need you to come with me – to sit in the parlour and be chaperone, whilst I talk to Lord Kevin."

The maid bobbed a curtsey, and followed her out of the room. She went down the stairs as slowly as she could force herself to – it would not do at all to look like an eager child, and run! But she wanted to run, silly fool that she was. When she reached the parlour door, Tomps was waiting. He opened it, and announced her. As she stepped into the room, Lord Kevin rose from the couch and came towards her. The sight of him took her breath away. The sun through the high windows drew strong reddish glints from his dark hair, and the simple elegance of his attire emphasised his lean powerful body. She had missed him badly, she realised, for this week that he had been away.

"Lord Kevin. It is a pleasure to see you, as always."

She went forward, and he took her hand for a moment, bowing. Even through her gloves, the heat of it rushed through her, leaving her flushed.

"My Lady, thank you for receiving me, when I have so rudely arrived on your doorstep with no prior warning."

"I assure you, it is of no matter – I am always happy to have the opportunity to converse with you. And I find that surprises are rarely unpleasant. Please, do resume your seat, and let us speak – for I assume that you are here for a reason?"

Sally had slipped in behind her, and gone to sit in the farthest corner of the room, in the window alcove, where the sun was warmest.

Greatly daring, she moved to sit on the empty space on the couch, next to where he had been sitting. He met her eyes, and raised an eyebrow as he dropped back to his seat. He was amused by her – again! Damn him!

"I must admit, Lady Hyacinth, that I am driven here by no great purpose – I have no shocking news to impart or such like. I am here because I felt the impulse to see you, after not having done so for a week. One might say that I am in need of bracing conversation."

Hyacinth regarded him, unsure, for the moment, of how to respond. Part of her was full of giddy delight, that he had come simply because he wanted to see her – no matter that he expressed it as simply a need for spirited conversation. But part of her was annoyed – was that all he saw in her – conversation to relieve his ennui? Well then, let her ensure that it was as sharp as possible.

"I see. And what topic might you wish to discuss, Lord Kevin? Fashion? The latest scandals? The importance of horticulture? Which ladies wield the most political influence, through their bedrooms?"

His smile widened, and then he laughed – an open joyous sound that vibrated in her very bones. The man confounded her – he was never shocked by anything she said, but he never ignored her words either. Once the laughter subsided, he regarded her with an almost sardonic smile on his full lips – lips which she found herself watching, all too closely. Heat flushed through her again, and she turned her eyes down.

"Delightful, as always. I am quite certain that your opinions on feminine political influence would be accurate, and enlightening."

Hyacinth blinked, amused in her turn.

"Ah, but did you not hear the important part of my suggestion – that the influence we might discuss is achieved in the bedroom? Or are you being delicately polite, because 'surely a gently reared young lady did not just say that'?"

"Oh, I heard it, most definitely. And no, I am not being delicately circumspect. I am, rather, widening the scope of the discussion – for, of a certainty, some of those liaisons which result in political influence occur in places far different from bedrooms."

Hyacinth felt herself blush, for her mind had, as she was quite sure that he had intended, immediately imagined other places in which such liaisons might, and almost certainly did, occur. How did he manage it, so easily? How did he turn her words back on her, as no other man ever had, and disconcert her so? And why did she enjoy it so much, even when it annoyed her?

She forced her thoughts to remembering gossip, rather than imagining the acts involved – she would not let him see how very much he disturbed her.

"Hmmm. I do believe that you are correct. I suspect, from what I have observed, that the studies, libraries, and even linen closets, of many great houses may well have been utilised in such a fashion. Certainly, the timing of the disappearance, and reappearance, of certain people at society Balls would suggest it is so. But you will need to observe it for yourself, and draw your own conclusions, my Lord."

He smiled that devilish smile, and, as if unaware of his actions, reached out and traced a finger down her arm.

She shivered in response, every part of her aware of the touch.

"What – surely you do not deny me the information which you so obviously have, on such matters? You titillate with hints, and leave me unsatisfied and guessing? You are, Lady Hyacinth, cruel in the extreme. I shall simply have to continue to ask you these utterly improprietous questions, until you reveal all of the sins of society to me."

"You will? How charmingly inappropriate of you. I, of course, will continue to behave as a respectable lady should, and deny all knowledge of such shocking matters. Thus, we have a conundrum, which may lead us to forever converse, without either of us actually providing the other with anything of substance. Which might, of course, be quite adequate to enliven our evenings, when in the presence of the *ton*."

"And perhaps our days as well, should I call upon you again – if you will permit me to do so, of course?"

Hyacinth felt a shiver of anticipation run through her – he wanted to spend more time with her, to call on her again! She wanted it, but she was not about to admit how very much.

"I might permit you to call – I do find our conversations amusing. There are very few gentlemen who are not disgusted by my forthrightness."

"Excellent – I shall take that as agreed – for I think that they are all mad, to be disgusted by what is simply a demonstration of intelligence. And the falseness and subterfuge which characterise so many conversations at social occasions I find quite exhausting, and a total waste of time. Bluntness is far more refreshing."

"I am glad that you find it so."

He smiled at her again, that smile that somehow left her feeling as if hot liquid slipped through her body, melting her a little, and she returned the smile, unable to help herself. Then he rose, and bowed.

"But I have taken up too much of your time, with this impromptu visit. I will leave you to the rest of your day, but I look forward to seeing you again, soon."

She rose also, and saw him to the door, her mind spinning. By soon, did he mean the Ball scheduled for that very evening?

She certainly hoped so.

<<<< O >>>>

Not long after Hyacinth had left the park, Abner Milne, Lord Puglinton, entered it through the gate on the other side of the square. He had been observing, since renting the house for the Season, the comings and goings of the other residents of the square. He had been most pleased to discover that the Duke of Elbury and his family resided there – and even more pleased when Lady Hyacinth had shown herself to have a tendency to spend time in the park – often, as far as he could see, shockingly alone.

When he had risen to find the day so warm and pleasant, he had decided to go to the park, in the hope that he might find Lady Hyacinth there. For whilst she might have a sharp tongue, as her reputation had suggested, she also had a very large dowry, and a figure that any man would appreciate. He wanted the money, and the body – and for that, he could ignore her opinions – surely, as a spinster nearing twenty-two years of age, she could not afford to spurn a suitor – no matter what she said.

And he needed an heir. His daughter was a nice enough child, but his first wife had died trying to bring his son into the world – and had failed, for the boy had died too. Lady Hyacinth seemed sturdy, and her breeding was impeccable. She would suit nicely.

He wandered the paths of the park, as casually as possible, intending to seem just a man out for a walk in the warmth of the late spring sun, but all the while checking every nook and cranny of the place, hoping to find her. She was not there. Not even in the most secluded spot in the park – that rather silly looking folly with the bench and the overgrowth of ivy. He paused beside the bench, repressing his annoyance.

As he did, something caught his eye – something out of place. He stepped closer to the bench, and peered at the tangle of ivy behind it. Yes, there was definitely something there – something which was not plant matter. The corner of what seemed a book peeked out from amongst the leaves, its dark red surface in strong contrast to the green around it. He sank to sit on the bench, and reached down to retrieve it. When he lifted it, some small thing fell from it, and clattered on the bench, before rolling away – the stub of a pencil.

He ignored it, and opened the book. It appeared to be a journal of some sort, although no name graced its first few pages anywhere. Instead, the first page showed a blotchy blueish thing – a child's attempt at watercolours – he had no idea what it was meant to be. If that was all it contained, it was a very dull find indeed. But Lord Puglinton was a curious man, and he had good reason to hope that he held something more interesting than a child's sketches. All thought of Lady Hyacinth left his mind.

Lord Puglinton had, for the last six months, been the primary owner of a newssheet ostentatiously titled 'The Society Commentator'. It was well known, and he was focussed on making it more so – and hence more profitable. For its main content was gossip – usually dressed up as serious articles, but always attempting to reveal the scandals of members of the *ton*, so that others of the *ton* could read them.

He was succeeding – the readership was growing, and the publication had become colloquially known as 'The Gossip Gazette' – a soubriquet which could only lead to even better sales. And if what he had found was a private journal of any kind, then it might be a treasure trove that he held, especially if he could discover who it belonged to. Almost salivating at the possibilities, he turned the pages, and began to read. Moments later, he slammed it shut with a small laugh which seemed on the edge of hysteria, and rose, tucking it into his coat.

Once home, and safely away from prying eyes, he spent hours reading it, from start to finish. He had, indeed, found a treasure – a treasure which would allow him to add a new column to the Commentator, and have material for it for many months to come. For the pages were filled with astute and very sharp-edged commentary on very recognisable figures of society – sometimes even named, to his utter glee – commentary which disparaged their attire, their attitudes and more, in a manner that he knew the aristocracy would find delightfully, scandalously entertaining.

He would begin to publish parts of it immediately – whilst he set about discovering just who had written it.

CHAPTER EIGHT

Hyacinth went up to her room after Lord Kevin had left, her mind in a daze. She told Sally to leave her be, that she would deal with the discarded day dress herself, for she wanted to be alone, to think. But, once she had turned the key in the lock, she realised that, so distracted had she been by Lord Kevin's presence, she had not thought to put her journal away in its place.

She flushed to think that, had she let Sally gather up the discarded dress, Sally might have found, and read, that journal. Really, she would need to be far more careful! She went to the bed, and lifted the dress, slipping her hand through the tangle of the skirts to find the pockets. When she did, she froze, the breath suddenly gone from her lungs – for the pockets were empty.

Fear filled her – where could it be? What if someone found it, and read it? She checked again – the pockets were still empty. Frantic now, she searched the room – had it fallen out onto the bed? Or the floor, when she had hastily discarded the dress?

But the room remained as it always was, and the journal was nowhere to be seen. Mentally, she retraced her steps – could it possibly have fallen out when she had rushed up the stairs to change? Worried, she unlocked the door, and walked carefully down the hallway, and down the steps, looking around her – no journal – everything was as immaculately in order as always, and there was no sign of anything out of place.

Hyacinth paused in the entryway, facing the only, most horrible conclusion – she had to have lost it in the park, or on the way back to the house. For, now that she thought of it, she had, as she'd risen from the bench, felt the tug as it dropped fully into the pocket, hadn't she? She was sure that she had. There was nothing for it, she had to go back to the park, and check every inch of the way there.

Tomps, impassive, stood in the entryway, ready to open whatever doors were required. Hyacinth squared her shoulders, and tried to look relaxed.

"I am just going to walk to the park and back – I feel the need of some fresh air."

Tomps face did not change, but she was certain that he thought her most odd. He opened the door for her, and watched as she walked slowly down the steps, along the footpath, and across the cobbles towards the park. Every step of the way, she studied the ground around her – but there was no sign of the journal, at all.

She went through the park gate, and along the paths towards the bench in the folly. There was no sign of it. Finally, she reached the bench, and stood there, her heart beating hard – what would she do, if she could not find it?

There was nothing on the bench. Hyacinth bent, and looked at the tangle of ivy surrounding it. Nothing.

But then, as she turned away, her foot twisted beneath her – she had stepped on some small thing. Righting herself, she bent to look. It was her pencil. She picked it up, and sank onto the bench, her mind reeling. What if... that tug had been her journal snagging slightly on her skirts as it fell out of her pocket, rather than deeper into it? The fact that the pencil was here gave credence to that idea.

And, if the pencil was here, then... the journal should be too, for the pencil had been tucked between its pages. Frantic, she pulled the ivy aside, scrabbling in the undergrowth all around the bench. Nothing. It wasn't there. She checked again. Definitely not there. She sat for a moment, barely holding herself calm. If the pencil was here, and the journal was not, then there was only one possibility that she could imagine – someone had found it.

As she walked slowly back to the house, she held one small thing to her as consolation – at least it did not have her name written in it.

<<<< O >>>>

As Hyacinth prepared for the Ball they were to attend that evening, the worry about her journal wore away at her. She felt irritable and frightened – for she had not found it, and the more she thought about it, the more she was sure that someone else had – but who?

By the time they left for the Ball, she was no closer to an answer. She fervently hoped that Lord Kevin would be at the Ball – she felt very much in need of distraction from her fear.

Once they arrived, she scanned the room, almost desperately, at the same time being darkly amused by her own behaviour – she had teased Lily for being smitten with Lord Canterford, but here she was, behaving just as Lily had! Was she smitten with Lord Kevin? The answer was most probably yes.

In that moment, she pushed the thought aside – even if she was, she wasn't going to behave like most silly women did! Then her eyes found him, at the other side of the room – she released the tension which had filled her – if Lord Kevin was here, then it was likely that Lord Puglinton would be less... attentive... to her.

Soon afterwards, Lord Kevin came to greet them, and she found herself walking about the room with him, conversing, as had become their habit. She knew that she was not as bright in manner, nor as sharp in her observations as usual, for the worry about the journal still affected her. She hoped that he would not notice. And, at first, he seemed not to. Until they danced.

<<<< O >>>>

"Lady Hyacinth, is aught amiss with you? You seem a little distant, a little distracted, tonight."

Kevin had been observing, as they had conversed, that she seemed out of sorts – her eyes clouded as if with some worry, and her commentary on those around them far less pointed than usual. It was so out of character that it worried him – and at the deepest part of himself, he wondered – did this have anything to do with his impetuous call upon her that afternoon? Had he offended her in some way? Suddenly, as they danced, he could not prevent himself from asking. She met his eyes, and a flicker of emotion passed across her face, before she gave a tiny shake of her head.

"No, my Lord, nothing is amiss. I am perhaps a little distracted by family matters. I strongly suspect that Lord Canterford is going to ask Lily to marry him. Which, whilst we will all be happy for her, will mean that our world will descend into the madness that will be my mother planning a wedding celebration."

He laughed – a gentle, almost conspiratorial laugh, for he understood her concerns, from a very personal perspective.

"Oh dear! I do understand. My mother is completely overwhelming when given the chance to arrange a wedding. As she will soon be doing for the second of my sisters. We shall have to commiserate with each other as it all happens."

She brightened a little, although something still seemed to dim her usual brilliance.

"We shall, indeed."

They danced on, and allowed a companionable silence to fall between them. Once the music ended, he took her back to her family, and stayed to speak with the Duke, whose opinions on life he was coming to value. That seemed to deter Lord Puglinton for the evening, and Kevin was glad – he was finding it harder and harder to watch Lady Hyacinth dance with any other man, though he had no right to feel that way.

When he returned to Chester House that night, the memory of that fleeting expression he had seen on her face haunted him. It was almost like it was with his father – he felt that something was wrong, yet he could not pin down exactly what it was. Over the next week or so, he saw her at multiple social events - they spoke, and danced, all much as they had before, yet that shadow was still there, dimming her brightness.

And Lord Puglinton was still attentive to her, in a way that made Kevin clench his jaw when he saw it. The desire to plant Puglinton a facer grew in him, every time he saw the man.

<<<< O >>>>

Lord Canterford had finally asked Lily to marry him! Elbury House was in uproar, and Hyacinth let all of the fuss draw her in, so that she managed not to think about the fate of her journal for whole hours at a time. Her mother had embraced Lily, when she had been told, then turned to Hyacinth with a smile.

"Well Hyacinth, after this, I will expect you to also find a good man to marry, and soon! You have waited far too long, as has Lily."

Hyacinth's mind had produced the image of Lord Kevin, and she had felt a slight heat rise into her cheeks.

"I make you no promises, Mama. You know that I will not marry anyone who does not truly care for me, or that I do not truly care for in return."

Her mother had nodded, but had then, mercifully, turned back to Lily, and begun discussing wedding gowns. Fortunately, that evening and the following one, there were no Balls or soirees to attend. Hyacinth was glad, even though it meant that she would not see Lord Kevin, for it also meant that she was able to avoid Lord Puglinton.

By mid-afternoon on the second day, Hyacinth was heartily sick of it all – and this was only the beginning! She had forced herself to be more involved, but she could only deal with it for so long at a time.

She excused herself from the discussion on what flowers should be used to decorate the ballroom for the wedding – a discussion which might last days, given her family – and went to sit in the library for a while, just for some quiet. Not long after, however, Marks, the butler, tapped on the door.

"Excuse me, Lady Hyacinth, but you have a caller."

He handed her the card. Lord Kevin. Her heart beat faster, and a smile came to her lips. She could not imagine a better distraction from the wedding madness which had overtaken her family.

"Please show him into the blue parlour – I think that is free of wedding… items…"

"Yes, my Lady."

Marks' eyes twinkled, although his face remained as impassive as ever. He understood his employer's family very well.

Hyacinth smoothed down her skirts, and made sure that the pins were not immediately about to fall out of her hair. Then she counted to twenty before she allowed herself to exit the room, and walk calmly to the blue parlour. When she entered, he was standing by the window, looking out at the sunlit street. The light from the window cast his profile into sharp relief, gilding him so brightly that he seemed some statue cast in gold. She paused, breathless, simply watching him.

As if he felt her eyes upon him, he turned, and a smile wreathed his face. He really was stunningly handsome when he smiled.

"Good day, Lord Kevin."

"Good day, Lady Hyacinth – I trust that I am not disturbing your day too badly?"

"On the contrary, I am most grateful for your arrival – for two days ago, Lord Canterford proposed to Lily, and she accepted. With a wedding to plan, my entire family have gone mad. Mother has waited years for the first of us to marry, and every bit of frustrated desire caused by that is being poured into planning. Your arrival rescues me from that, at least for the duration of your visit."

His eyes met hers, full of amusement, and warmth filled her.

"Then may I suggest that I remove you from it completely, at least for an hour or two? The day is beautiful, and I have driven my phaeton, in the hope of convincing you to allow me to take you for a drive through Hyde Park. It is a pleasant vehicle, not too high-perch, and has a seat, admittedly small, at the back, which will allow your maid to come with us, for propriety's sake. Might you be persuaded?"

"I might indeed. That sounds delightful. Allow me a few minutes to change into an appropriate gown, and to fetch my maid."

"Certainly. I will await your return."

He bowed, his eyes still full of amusement, and she nodded, before hurrying out of the parlour, and up the stairs. It was, she thought, probably the fastest that she had ever changed clothes! When attired suitably, in a rich blue carriage dress and carrying a fur trimmed pelisse, in case the day should unexpectedly turn cold, she tied a bonnet decorated with small blue feathers over her hair, and went back downstairs to ask Marks to tell the family where she was going.

She rather thought that her mother would barely notice, as soon as she was assured that Sally would go with her.

When she entered the parlour, his expression told her that he liked the way that she looked, and pleased warmth blossomed inside her. Whilst she did not aspire to being the height of fashion, she did always try to look her best. He came to her, and offered his arm. She placed her hand upon it. He waved in the direction of the door.

"Shall we go?"

"Yes. I see no reason to delay, and if I am not here, I cannot get pulled back into the wedding planning."

He laughed softly, and led her out, Sally following them closely.

Outside, Tomps was at the horses' heads, and the team of matched chestnuts stood quietly, dozing in the sun. Lord Kevin helped Sally up into the small groom's seat at the rear of the phaeton. Sally looked at him nervously.

"You won't go too fast now, my Lord, will you?"

"I won't, Sally. I'm not one for racing about to no purpose – we'll just have a peaceful drive in the sunshine."

"Thank you, my Lord."

The maid blushed, knowing that she had been very forward in asking – but somehow, Lord Kevin seemed to inspire confidence in people. He turned back to Hyacinth, and assisted her up onto the high seat of the phaeton, then swung up beside her in a fluid movement that spoke of long practice, and the strength of a very fit man.

It seemed most improbable that she should be here, being driven by a gentleman, simply for the pleasure of it, yet here she was. She did not speak, as they worked their way through the busy streets towards Hyde Park, leaving him all of his concentration for driving through the traffic. Instead, she simply watched him, appreciating his skill.

Hyde Park was not as crowded as she might have expected, given the lovely day, but they were somewhat earlier than the hour at which the *ton* tended to come out to see and be seen. For which she was grateful – suddenly, she was nervous about what people might say, seeing her being driven out by Lord Kevin. Internally, she chided herself for foolishness – in the past, she had worked hard to stop worrying about what others thought of her – why was she doing so now?

Once in the Park, he set the horses to a steady walk, and turned his attention more to Hyacinth.

"So, now that we are safely distanced from the chaos of wedding planning, what shall we discuss, my Lady?"

She looked at him a moment, then at the other riders and carriages in the Park, and the small groups picnicking on the grass in some areas. Out of habit, she considered their attire, and who was with whom and all of the little things that she would write in her journal later. And then she swallowed hard. She could not write in her journal, for it was gone. The day seemed to dim around her, and she tried her best to stop thinking of it. At least, with Lord Kevin, she could say what she thought of the people around them.

"I do believe, my Lord, that those of the *ton* who are out today are as... talented... in their choice of attire as any."

"Oh? Does anyone in particular lead you to that conclusion?"

"Well... over there," she indicated with a wave of her hand, and he turned to look in that direction, "The group riding along the path towards the Serpentine – the gentleman on the bright chestnut horse – I fear that the brightness of his horse's coat has made him feel inadequately noticeable – for he seems to have chosen attire which is designed, by the fact of its many clashing colours and patterns, to render the horse barely noticeable by comparison. And that lace... all blowing in the breeze!"

"Indeed, I find that my eyes hurt, simply looking at the man. I sometimes wonder if these people choose such outrageous things, just so that others will gossip about them, as if notoriety was something to be sought."

"I suspect that they do – but it is a foolish choice - for with gossip, one can never tell whether it will be vicious and destructive to a person's reputation, or simply sharp and lightly mocking. I may make very sharp-edged observations, but it has never been my habit to share them – until you tempted me into these dreadfully improper conversations. I would not like to see my words repeated, and exaggerated, or used to hurt someone."

"That is a very wise attitude, Lady Hyacinth. And I thank you for the trust that you have placed in me, by allowing these delightful discussions between us. Sadly, it seems that others are not so sensibly reticent. I went to my club yesterday, and all that everyone could talk about was a new column in that newssheet – the Society Commentator – the one they call the 'Gossip Gazette'. It seems that the paper has sunk to a new low with this column, and people are not sure how to react."

"Oh? In what way? I admit that I have never looked at it – it is not the kind of publication that I choose to read."

"Well, apparently, the articles are thinly disguised mockery of various members of society, and in some cases have brought back to public view some scandals thought forgotten more than a year ago. Some people are amused, others seem more worried – perhaps they have their own scandals that they wish to see stay hidden?"

Hyacinth fought to keep her expression bland, but a horrible suspicion had blossomed in her mind. A new column, that yet touched on old scandals, as well as more recent commentary... could it be...

"I see. When did this start – for I gather that it is quite recent, or I would expect to have heard whispers about it?"

"Only a few days ago, I believe, but the contents are pointed, and apparently accurate enough to have set them all talking."

Horror filled her. If someone had found her journal, and was using it to create articles to publish... she swallowed hard. She needed to obtain a copy of this publication, and see for herself – she could not rest until she was certain of the truth. For now, she could not reveal anything, lest Lord Kevin suspect that something was wrong. He was too observant, too likely to notice if she allowed her manner to change.

"Some people will talk to anyone, about anything, whether it is real, or utterly fictitious. But let us speak of something else."

<<<< O >>>>

Kevin watched Lady Hyacinth. He was quite certain that something was wrong, though she did her best to hide it.

When he had described the articles in the Gossip Gazette she had stilled, her normally animated face assuming a somewhat fixed expression. He had expected her to be somewhat dismissive of the gossip sheet – for he had known, even before she had put it into words, that her sharp observations were kept generally to herself, and only shared with a very few people, mainly her family. The tawdry spreading of gossip was simply not a thing that she would countenance.

Instead, she had looked, for an instant before her face had assumed that bland expression, almost horrified, or perhaps afraid? But what would cause such a reaction? Surely there was nothing in her life which she might fear to see end up in a gossip column? Her shrewish reputation was not on such a scale as to be scandalous enough to merit mention, when so many others in society were so much more worthy of featuring in such a publication.

But when she seemed uncomfortable with the topic, and asked to speak of something else, he willingly turned the conversation to other matters.

"Something else? I assume that means, other than weddings, and the madness that they induce in families?"

"It does. I think that we will both have quite enough of that in the near future. For you said that your second sister was about to marry?"

"Yes – Maria was widowed, more than a year ago. It was a very unpleasant time – with quite a bit of scandal mongering around it. But she has recovered, and will now marry a man who has loved her his whole life – Charles Barrington, Viscount Wareham."

Hyacinth thought a moment.

"So, your two sisters will have married brothers? Wareham is the Duke of Melton's brother, is he not?"

"Yes, he is. He is a quiet man, very skilled at matters of estate management, a proponent of modern farming methods and improving conditions for tenant farmers and workers. Both my father and I have learnt a lot, from observing what he has done for the Melton estates."

"You are interested in the detail of the management of your estates? Many gentlemen do not seem to care for such things."

"I am. Although I hope that the day when I become Viscount Chester is a long way off, I intend to fulfil my responsibilities well when I must."

She nodded, seeming pleased by his words, and they spoke a little longer about the changes in farming, and the need for the aristocracy to adapt, if their estates were to stay profitable, then, as the Park began to fill up with members of the *ton*, come to socialise, he turned the phaeton back towards Elbury House.

CHAPTER NINE

That evening, Hyacinth was more glad than ever that there was no social event to attend. After dinner, of which she ate very little, she claimed a megrim and retired to her room. Over and over, her mind replayed Lord Kevin's words about the column in the 'Gossip Gazette'. The dreadful sense that, somehow, her journal had become the material for that column would not leave her. In the morning, she would have to find a way to see a copy for herself. A way that did not involve any of her family, or the main household staff, discovering that she had it. Quite how she would achieve that, she did not know.

Sleep was slow in coming, and when it did, it was disturbed by strange dreams, so much so that when she woke, she felt as if she had barely rested at all. Nonetheless, she made herself rise, and rang for Sally to help her dress for the day. Once dressed, she stood at her window, and gazed down at the garden at the rear of the house, where the little gate led out into the mews at the back, and their stables. The day was beautiful – almost mockingly so.

As she watched, one of the stableboys came out of the stables, and through the gate, moving towards the kitchen door. Hyacinth nibbled on her lip, an idea coming to her. After a moment, with a decisive nod, she gathered up a few coins from where they lay in her drawer, and went downstairs.

She slipped out into the garden through the quiet house, only then realising how much earlier than usual she had woken, and wandered among the flowerbeds. Not long after, Tom, the stableboy, came back down the path from the kitchen. Hyacinth stepped forward.

"Tom."

"Yes, milady?"

"Might you do an errand for me?"

"An errand, milady?"

"Yes, I want to get a copy of a newssheet, without anyone else knowing."

The boy looked at her, and a slow smile spread across his face.

"Secrets, is it, milady? I'm good at keepin' secrets. What is it you wants a copy of?"

"Its called 'The Society Commentator' But I think that everyone calls it 'The Gossip Gazette'. I want a copy from one of the last three days."

"It'll be a few pence t'buy, milady..."

Hyacinth smiled, and handed him the coins she had brought. There was significantly more than the cost of the newssheet, she knew.

"The rest is for you, for your trouble."

"Thankee, milady. I'll be off then – you come back out t' the garden in an hour or two, and I'll have it for ye."

Hyacinth nodded, and the boy gave her an exaggerated bow, before running off, out through the gate and down the laneway.

The following two hours seemed to last forever. She went in, settled in the library with a book, and called for tea and biscuits – the idea of going to the breakfast room, and eating anything more substantial was just not something that she could contemplate. She sipped the tea, and attempted to read, but did not really succeed – she found herself reading the same page, over and over. She tried another book, but it held her interest even less. In the end, she simply sat, half dozing after her poor night's sleep, as the mantel clock ticked inexorably slowly through the required time. Its soft chime startled her back to awareness, and she rose, yawning, and so very glad that it was time to return to the garden.

Not long after she had stepped onto the shady path beyond the rose beds, the boy slipped through the gate, and came towards her. As he did, he removed something folded from his rather ragged looking shirt, and held it by his side. He paused when he reached her, and dipped a little bow, then moved on, surreptitiously handing her the folded paper as he did.

To anyone looking on, it would look as if he had simply politely acknowledged her as he went to the servants' door. She did not look at the tightly folded paper – she simply put it carefully into her pocket, bent and sniffed at the roses for a moment, then turned, and went back into the house, and up to her room.

Once inside, with the door locked, she drew it out, and unfolded the newssheet. It was printed on flimsy, poor quality paper, but the text was clear enough. There, down one side of the page, was a column labelled 'The Voice of Truth' – a headline which was enough to make her laugh, so improbable was it that one might normally find anything approaching truth in a scandal sheet.

She began to read the words below the heading, and as she did, she felt dizzy, icy cold, her head spinning, almost as if she was about to faint – and Hyacinth never, ever, fainted! The words were hers – this particular set of words being something that she had written, perhaps two months ago. Her words had been changed a little, to make things sound more scandalous than they were, but still, it was easy to recognise the characters involved, and the core of truth in it.

This particular piece was about Lady Gosham and Lord Bessmark. Hyacinth cast the dreadful thing into the fire, and curled into a little ball on her bed, shaking. Someone had found the journal, and her worst fears, indeed even worse than her worst fears, had come true. They were using her journal as material for the 'Gossip Gazette' – and if they published one piece a day, that journal still held enough material to keep them going for near a year.

No one knew that she had written those words, but, eventually, someone might begin to look around them, to work out who might have been present at all of the events which an article had been written about. And if they did, would they remember Lady Hyacinth, of the shrewish tongue and sharp-edged comments? Quite likely they would. No proof would be needed – just the rumoured suspicion would be enough.

Enough to destroy her, and her sisters, by association.

She cried then, a sound of hopeless despair, for she could see no way to stop this, no way to prevent things going on, until someone worked it out. She had been a fool – she had allowed herself to think that taking the journal to the park was reasonable, and then she had compounded her foolishness by being such a flutterhead about Lord Kevin coming to call, that she had not ensured that the journal was safe when she had left the park.

She would never write down her observations again. She would have to find some other way to get them out of her mind, to relieve the incessant pressure, which otherwise led her to speak her thoughts unwisely. But no amount of resolution to be more sensible in future could change what had already happened. Now, at every event, she would most likely hear people speak of the gossip column, and would need to dissemble, to hide her reactions. To never, ever, give the slightest clue that she might have possibly had anything to do with those articles being written.

<<<< O >>>>

Lord Puglinton sat at his desk, the red leather journal in his hands. It really had been the most wonderful find. The new column was gaining more interest from the readers every day, and sales were nearly twice what they had been, two weeks ago. The journal contained a lot of material – enough to keep the column going for some months – but not forever. Which meant that discovering who had written that journal had become imperative. He would not allow this boost to his wealth to falter, now that it had begun. Which meant that more material needed to be written.

So far, he had come to the conclusion that the writer was almost certainly a member of the aristocracy – for who else could have been in all of the right places to have seen the things that the journal entries recorded? Quite why they might have recorded all of their cynical and somewhat sarcastic views of their peers in a journal escaped him – but he did not care. All that mattered was that they had done so.

He thought, perhaps, that the writer was a woman. For the writing, even though done in pencil rather than ink, showed a flowing style more common to women than men, in his experience. In addition, the journalist commented, often, on the foibles of feminine fashion, in a way that he suspected few men would be capable of. But that did not exactly narrow the field of possibilities very far.

He turned it over again, searching it for any sign of a name, but there was none – nothing to indicate ownership. Perhaps that had been wise, and intentional on the part of the writer. But it was a damnable inconvenience for him. Surely, there was something about it to give him a clue. He looked at it again, paying close attention.

The leather exterior was no help, bearing nothing beyond the scuffs and scratches of years of handling. The first pages, where one might normally expect a person to write their name, bore no writing – only those childish watercolour blotches. He wondered, as he looked at them, if the person who had painted them as a child was the adult who had written in the journal, in such biting indictments of society. Was there a clue in those blotches?

He eyed them again – what were they meant to represent?

He allowed his eyes to unfocus a little, and to simply take in the whole impression, rather than looking at detail. The blotches, viewed that way, looked a little like... flowers? The sort of flowers that were a cluster of tiny blossoms around an upright stalk. If that was what they were meant to be, what did that tell him, if anything? Girls painted flowers all the time.

Perhaps the type of flower mattered? He knew that he was grasping at the veriest tiny threads here, but still, it was worth considering everything – for finding the writer was a prize worth the annoyance of this. He was by no means well educated on the types of flowers in existence, beyond the existence of roses and such like, which one might give to a lady, so attempting to remember the names of flowers was a great struggle.

What sorts of flowers looked like that – an upright stick with a cluster of small blossoms around it? Hollyhocks? Not quite right. Foxglove? No. Lupins? They were often that blueish colour – did the colour matter? Snapdragon? None of them, from the faint memories he had of being told which flower was which, seemed quite right. What other flowers were blue? Perhaps the colour was the most significant – after all, children tended to be very direct in their attempts to replicate the world around them.

None came to mind. Irritated, he closed the journal and locked it away in his desk. He would think on it more, later. For now, he needed to eat, and then prepare for the Ball he was to attend that night. Perhaps Lady Hyacinth would be there, and he could spend some more time convincing her that she should marry – preferably him. She might have a sharp tongue, but that dowry... Lady Hyacinth was ...

Hyacinth....

He stopped, and sat there, breathing hard.

Hyacinth. A blue flower, which consisted of a collection of tiny blossoms around a central stalk.

Lady Hyacinth Gardenbrook. A woman with a sharp tongue and a rather cynical view of those around her. A woman who lived across the square, and whom he had seen spend time in the park. The park he had gone to, hoping to meet her, on the day when he had found the journal.

Was it possible? Had he been spending time with the writer of all of this wonderful gossip, for months, without knowing it? The more that he thought about it, the more logical it seemed, the more obvious – and the more delightful.

For he would no longer need to gently persuade her of anything. With this, he could almost certainly blackmail her into doing whatever he wanted. For if she was revealed as the writer of the column, she would become a pariah in the eyes of society – they did not like those who betrayed their own – gossip whispered in corners was accepted – gossip published in scandal sheets was another matter entirely. And if she was spurned, so would her sisters be. He was quite sure that Lady Hyacinth would do the noble thing, to protect her sisters.

As he thought about it, he realised that her writing was of more value to him, even, than her dowry would be. For if she could write an endless amount of this gossip about the *ton*, fuelled by her ongoing observations of them, it would make him far more money than even her dowry, over time, if the circulation of the Society Commentator continued to increase as it had since he had first printed the 'Voice of Truth' column.

Smiling, he went to prepare for the evening.

<<<< O >>>>

Hyacinth was beginning to be rather over going to Balls – but the Season was slowing towards its close, as May moved into June, and the days got ever warmer. She stood in the ballroom at Porthaven House, and looked at the assembled people. Were they whispering about the 'Voice of Truth' gossip column? Were they looking at everyone present, wondering who wrote those articles?

She shivered at the thought, feeling exposed, and terribly alone. Lord Kevin was not there. Yet again, he had disappeared, with no word to her. All of her doubts about him resurfaced – did he have a mistress somewhere? She shook her head – what business of hers was it if he did? No matter that she liked him, there was nothing formal between them. People milled around her, talking to her parents, and to her sisters. Lily and Lord Canterford stood in the midst of a group of people, all of whom were congratulating them on their betrothal. Hyacinth felt somehow isolated amongst them, as if she was not quite, truly, present.

"Lady Hyacinth – it's delightful to see you tonight. You will grant me this dance, won't you?"

Lord Puglinton stood before her, his smile reminiscent of a wolf regarding a rabbit, and the tone of his words indicating that he did not expect her to do anything except comply. Her sense of despair deepened. She could not, now more than ever, afford to create a scene. She set her expression into her best bland social mask, and placed her hand on his proffered arm.

"Of course, Lord Puglinton. I trust that you are well?"

The most basic of conversation seemed safest.

91

"Very well indeed, Lady Hyacinth, the more so because you are here this evening."

Hyacinth looked at him, wondering why he was so cheerful, so much more so than normal. They took their places in the line, as the orchestra began to play, and she allowed herself to simply follow the steps, attempting to speak as little as possible. His lips twisted into a smile again – a smile that seemed mocking, somehow.

"Lady Hyacinth, you seem most subdued this evening – have you nothing to say? Or are you turning your excellent powers of observation upon those around you, so assiduously that you have not time for speech?"

His words chilled her – what was he implying? He couldn't possibly know... could he?

The dance spun them around, then brought them back together to promenade down between the lines. When they reached the end, instead of spinning her out so that they each joined the lines again, he tugged her onwards, and all but dragged her out through the doors onto the terrace above the garden.

"Lord Puglinton! What..."

"Shhh. You will find out soon enough." He pulled her along the terrace, until they stood at the far end, well enough away from the doors to not be easily overheard. "I think, Lady Hyacinth, that you are hiding a secret."

"A secret? What on earth do you mean?"

Her heart beat thunderously against her ribs, and fear shot through her - did he know?

Puglinton laughed.

"You can pretend all you like, Lady Hyacinth, but I am quite sure that you are the author of all of that delightful gossip. The style is so similar to the way that you speak, when you attempt to deliver a set down. That red leather journal was a most serendipitous find."

Her fists clenched at her sides, and for a moment, she could not breathe. He did know. He had her journal – and, somehow, he was responsible for its publication.

"I don't know what you are speaking of."

She cursed herself inwardly at the slight shake in her voice.

Puglinton laughed again, and it was not a pleasant sound.

"My dear Lady, I can see that you know exactly what I am speaking of, even if you deny it. So, let me be blunt, as you are so fond of being. I want something from you. Preferably yourself, as a wife. But, if you are unwise enough to wish to remain a spinster, then there is another option, at least for a while – I may come back to marriage later, when perhaps you will have tired of being alone. I want you to continue to write your delightful commentaries on society – as many of them as you can produce, as fast as you can produce them. In return, I will agree not to reveal you as the author. I am quite certain that the doyennes of society would not be forgiving – especially as my editor has... enhanced... some of your stories a little. And you would not want your sisters' reputations to suffer, would you – even if you care nothing for your own?"

Hyacinth forced herself to be still, for anything she said would almost certainly confirm everything to him.

"Nothing to say? I will allow you that, tonight. But I will not give you more than four weeks to give me your answer. In four weeks, if you have not agreed to my offer, in one way or another, then I will expose you as the writer, in the most shocking way that I can manage." He bowed to her, mockingly, with an excessive flourish. "Good evening Lady Hyacinth. Do enjoy the rest of the Ball."

CHAPTER TEN

Kevin sat with his father in the study at Chester Park, tiredness filling him. He had not intended to be back here so soon, yet his mother had sent a letter, begging that he come home for at least a few days, to help with all of the organising for Charles and Maria's wedding. Why it took so much, when they had intentionally chosen to have a quiet wedding in the nearby small church, he was not quite sure, but he had come as she had asked.

Lord Chester looked more careworn than ever, and seemed, somehow, to have shrunk somewhat since Kevin had seen him last, but a few weeks before. Kevin rose, and went to the sideboard, filling two glasses from the brandy decanter. As he replaced the stopper in the decanter, an odd choked sound came from behind him. He spun around, to see his father hastily wiping his lips with a handkerchief. A handkerchief which was spotted with blood. In two steps, Kevin was beside Lord Chester, his hand halting his father's as the older man tried to shove the stained handkerchief into a pocket.

"Father... that makes it obvious that, as I had suspected, something is very much amiss with you. Please, tell me the truth of it. Why have you hidden this?"

Lord Chester sighed, and Kevin stepped back, then retrieved the glasses of brandy, and sat down beside him again. His father sipped his brandy, and Kevin waited, hoping that he would get truth, not avoidance.

"Why have I hidden it? Because this is a time for Maria to be happy, for her to marry, and go to have a life of her own with a man who will be good to her. You know your sister – if she knew that I ailed in any way, she would be brewing healing tisanes and refusing to leave here until she either healed me, or I was gone from this earth. That's no life for a young woman who has already suffered enough! I am quite sure that this can't be healed, anyway. My grandfather went this way, and I watched the progression of the disease. I don't know how long I have, but I doubt it's more than a year, at most. So, I have been putting my affairs in order, preparing things so that it will be as easy as possible for you, when you must take up the responsibilities of the title."

Kevin felt his heart sink. He had hoped... but no, in the core of him, he had known, for a long time now, that what was amiss with his father was something like this. He had simply not wanted to believe it.

"Will you at least see a physician, and confirm the truth of it – you could be wrong about it not being able to be healed."

"Perhaps – but not until after Maria and Charles are wed, and gone off to the north – Melton's giving them that northernmost property as a wedding gift, did you know?"

"I didn't know – that is generous of him, and I did know that Charles had wanted to start a business in woollen mills in that area. But you attempt to distract me from the matter at hand. You must take the best care of yourself that you can, until we can get you to a physician at least. If I must spend even more time here, to get everything done, then I will, although... there are a few matters in London that I cannot completely abandon."

In his mind Kevin considered those matters – the foremost of which was, he had to admit, one Lady Hyacinth Gardenbrook. What would his father think of Lady Hyacinth, he wondered?

"I'll be all right, I've done well enough until now, I can continue to do so. Even your mother doesn't realise how serious this is – thankfully, she's thoroughly distracted by the wedding preparations. You do what you need to do, but prepare – for when I do go, you'll certainly have a lot to deal with, in that first few months."

"Please, do not speak of it so – I am not yet ready to believe that you are doomed to leave us, and so soon."

"Best get used to it, my boy – whether you want it to be true or not, I know that it is."

They dropped into silence, and drank perhaps more brandy than was wise, Kevin was at a loss – what could he do, when his father had accepted his apparent fate with such equanimity? He wanted someone to talk to, to unburden his soul to – and he had no one who was that close to him. At that thought, the image of Lady Hyacinth rose in his mind, with the odd certainty that she would understand, and listen. But she was in London, and he was here.

That night, as he went to bed, he felt lonelier than ever before.

<<<< O >>>>

Lily's wedding went off perfectly – much to the Duchess' delight. Hyacinth was simply relieved – now she stood in the ballroom at Elbury House, talking to a group of people, which included the Duke and Duchess of Melton, Lord Kevin, and a few others that she barely knew. Her mother had made the wedding the event of the Season, and invited almost the entirety of the *ton*, it seemed.

Lord Kevin had been there, at the church, and Hyacinth had felt a rush of relief at seeing him. Somehow, just his presence made her feel stronger. For Lord Puglinton's ultimatum echoed in her mind, every time that she paused long enough to allow thought to happen. She shivered, remembering it again – here she was, miserable, and afraid, in a room full of people who were all celebrating the obvious happiness of Lily and her new husband with great cheer.

She felt almost disloyal to Lily, for not being happy at her sister's wedding, yet she could not stop the feeling, could not stop the fear. What answer could she give Lord Puglinton? For she had no doubt that he would do as he had threatened, and expose her to the *ton*, if she did not at least partly comply with his wishes.

She kept her false smile on her face, and let her thoughts wander. There was no way that she could find, to not think about Lord Puglinton, the journal, and her predicament. Lord Kevin glanced her way often, but said nothing. She almost wished that he would speak, for she was close to certain that he knew that something was wrong, for her.

Then the dancing began, and he offered her his arm.

She took it – they understood each other well enough now that he did not need to ask. He led her to the floor, and into place, as the waltz began. Only once they had been moving for some minutes did he say anything.

"Lady Hyacinth, what is wrong? For I am certain that something is. You seem quiet and withdrawn, yet I know that you are happy for your sister – you are not concerned about her marriage – so it must be something else."

For a moment, she had the impulse to tell him everything.

She stopped herself. Telling anyone would only increase the risk of it all coming out. And there was no point – what could anyone do to help her? Nothing. She was in this situation because of her own actions, and she would have to deal with the consequences. Even if she refused to marry Lord Puglinton – and she would, for the idea revolted her – she would still be forced to keep writing articles for him, just to protect her sisters. And, as he had intimated, he could choose, at any stage in the future, to insist on the marriage – he held all of the power. She felt rather like a mouse, played with by a cat, simply for its amusement.

How could she prevent him from demanding marriage, later? Her mind tumbled around the question, even as she smiled at Lord Kevin.

"I am fine, my Lord – but the last few weeks have exhausted me, with all of the preparations. I fear that I am not good company at present."

He raised an eyebrow, his eyes concerned, and she knew that he did not believe her excuse. That knowledge warmed her heart, even as it left her afraid.

Her mind went back to the matter of ensuring that Lord Puglinton could never demand that she marry him. The thought came, that really, there was only one way that could be made impossible – and that was if she was already married to another man. A tiny gasp escaped her.

Lord Kevin met her eyes, and she felt that she could drown in their deep brown depths. *If I should have to marry, in haste, this is the man I would choose*. The thought happened without any conscious intent on her part. It floated there in her mind, an idea that left her even more breathless. *But why would he even consider such a thing? I do not know that he even cares for me, beyond our rather odd friendship...* yet she could not easily dismiss the idea.

It seemed the single hope she had of any advantage in the matter.

She pushed it aside. Later, if such a thing became her only desperate hope, then maybe, if she was brave, she might ask him – but she was not certain that she was that brave, at all.

<<<< O >>>>

Kevin knew that she had lied to him – what he did not understand was why. She looked so sad, amongst all of the happiness of her sister's wedding, and his heart ached – he wanted to take that sadness away, to fix whatever was causing it.

But she was stubborn, would not admit it, would not tell him – just as his father had been, for so long.

As they danced, he had wanted, so very badly, to lower his head to hers, and kiss her, to kiss away the sadness, until she smiled properly again. But he had done nothing of the sort.

They were in a very public situation, and such an act would ruin her reputation on the instant, and likely lead to them being forced to marry.

Which was, he realised, not an unpleasant thought at all. He pushed the idea away as foolish – he did not know how she felt about him, beyond a most unusual friendship, and he would not risk that friendship by doing anything inappropriate.

They danced on, and Kevin cursed, internally, the timing of everything. He was worried about his father, Charles and Maria's wedding would happen in just two weeks' time, and he had to be back at Chester Park within days, as a result. Yet he wanted to stay here, to see Lady Hyacinth as often as possible, to discover what it was, that had dimmed her bright nature so much.

When the dance ended, and he escorted her to where her family were gathered, leaving her there and walking away was the hardest thing he had ever done.

<<<< O >>>>

Three days later, back at Chester Park, that sadness on Lady Hyacinth's face haunted him. He tried to ignore it, for there was nothing he could do – he would go back to London for a few days, then be back here again for Maria's wedding. Until then, there was nothing he could do, nothing at all. Best that he concentrated, instead, on helping his father, and attempting to persuade him to see a physician sooner.

In the evening, he sat in the study with his father again, as had become their habit, nursing a brandy as they spoke of his life in London, and of the estates, and a wide range of other things.

"In London, the latest subject of gossip, is gossip, mad though that sounds."

"What on earth do you mean?"

"Well, there is scandal sheet – ostentatiously called 'The Society Commentator' but which everyone has taken to calling 'The Gossip Gazette'. Have you heard of it?"

"I have. There was some bad business with that one, a year or so ago, if I remember aright. It used to be more of a respectable newssheet, but the man who owned most of it ran into trouble, with gambling, or some such, and the 'Commentator' changed hands. I assumed that it had been used to pay off a debt. But there were rumours – which suggested that the card games involved had been rigged in some way, that the man had been set up to lose. He lost everything, and left the country to escape his other debtors. Very bad business that. But no one ever proved anything, that I know of, and the new owner has made it much more of a scurrilous scandal sheet than anything else. What has he done now, to make it the talk of the town?"

"A week or two ago, it began running a new daily column – called something ridiculous like the 'Voice of Truth' – which features very sharp and sarcastic articles, based on the very real scandals of the aristocracy – the kind of thing that no one wants paraded on a newssheet. They are too close to the truth for anyone to like, although there are those who are titillated by such things. So the gossip spreads. No one knows who writes the column. And that intrigues them all, even more."

His father snorted with laughter.

"You'd think they'd all have better things to worry about."

CHAPTER ELEVEN

London was stifling, after Chester Park, the late spring weather as warm as summer. And that made the crowded ballroom positively sweltering. Nonetheless, Kevin was glad to be there. It was a relief, after the twin strains at Chester Park, of being cheerful about the wedding planning, whilst worrying more every day about his father's health. And, of course, there was the hope of seeing, and conversing with, Lady Hyacinth.

He was standing, as he so often did, in a quiet corner of the room – as much as anywhere could be quiet – and observing. From one Ball to the next, little seemed to change – the crowds of young women in their pastel gowns, the clusters of older women in outdated gowns, the men who were looking to choose a wife, and the men who most definitely had no interest in marriage. The cast never changed – all that shifted was who was talking to, and about, who.

The more time he spent with Lady Hyacinth, the more he found all of it utterly dull – unless she was there. And she was. She had just arrived, with her family.

Kevin straightened, and watched as they made their way into the room, greeted by many of those present. He forced himself to wait, until the family had chosen a spot to stand, and the first rush of people going to speak to them had slowed. No matter how much he wished to simply charge across the room to Lady Hyacinth, he was not about to do anything so impetuous.

However, as he waited, and watched, concern filled him. Lady Hyacinth seemed even more withdrawn than she had been before he had gone to Chester Park. She stood there, but she was not talking to anyone, and her expression was dull, and almost sad. He was moving before he had time to think about it, no longer able to stay away.

But, before he reached her, Lord Puglinton was greeting her. When Puglinton went to take her hand, bowing, Kevin was quite sure that she flinched – physically flinched – away from him. There was something very wrong there. Lady Hyacinth did not flinch from anything, in his experience of her. The movement was corrected almost immediately, and he doubted that anyone else had noticed – but he had, because he had been watching her so closely.

Puglinton led her over to where people were forming up for the next dance, and Kevin clenched his jaw, filled with a desperate desire to push through the crowds around him, to rush to her side, to somehow rescue her from Puglinton. But... did she need rescuing? Or was that just his rather selfishly biased view of the situation? He did not know, but he resolved to ask her, as soon as he could. At least, with Lady Hyacinth, he could do that – simply ask, bluntly, and she would not be offended that he did so.

Casually, he went to her family, and greeted them.

The Duke cheerfully launched into a discussion of farming practices, and the innovations in greenhouses which had been made in recent years. Kevin was genuinely interested, for the Duke of Elbury was a very knowledgeable man – and it gave him an excuse to be right there, when Lord Puglinton escorted Lady Hyacinth back to her family, as propriety demanded he do.

Lord Puglinton glared at Kevin as he approached with Lady Hyacinth, and Kevin smiled at the odious man, as if he cared not one whit what he did. Puglinton bowed stiffly, released Lady Hyacinth, and moved off. Lady Hyacinth, as if unaware of her actions, moved until she stood close to Kevin. So close that he became aware that she was quivering. He turned to her.

"Lady Hyacinth – I trust that you are well tonight, even though the heat in this ballroom is sufficient to cause one to feel faint."

Her eyes met his, and they seemed to be filled with some unspoken anguish.

"I am well enough Lord Kevin, although I must agree with you – it is quite stifling in here."

"Will you walk with me, a little? Perhaps the terrace is cooler?"

He offered her his arm, and she placed her hand on it, her fingers tightening, far more so than normal.

"I will, thank you. Perhaps there is a breeze outside."

The Duke had observed this exchange and nodded pleasantly at Kevin as they moved away towards the doors. Kevin was beyond glad that Lady Hyacinth's father appeared to trust his daughter with him, without hesitation.

They did not speak as they moved around the edge of the room, and Lady Hyacinth appeared to barely notice the people around them – which for her, was most unusual. Once they had reached the doors, and stepped out onto the terrace, she seemed to relax a little. He led her to a bench which was set at the far end of the paved terrace, hoping that the distance from the doors might provide a little privacy. She sank down onto the seat beside him, and stared out at the moonlit garden.

"Lady Hyacinth?"

She started, just a little, as if she had been deep in thought, and turned to face him.

"I am sorry, Lord Kevin, I am a little distracted this evening."

"That I can see. I am about to do something which may be foolish, but I trust that you know me well enough by now to accept my bluntness." Her face filled with confusion, but she said nothing, waiting for him to go on. "Lady Hyacinth, I am quite sure that there is a problem of some sort, between you, and Lord Puglinton. I noticed, even if no one else did, the way that you flinched away from his touch when he greeted you. Please – tell me the truth of it – has he stepped beyond the bounds of propriety in some way?"

Expressions flitted across her face – so rapidly that he could not quite tell what each was. Then she gave a little shake of her head.

"No. It is nothing like that. It is just that... he wants to marry me – and he seems to think that I should be glad of that. He is persistent, yet I find him odious. He does not accept my rejection of his suit, no matter how often I tell him that I am not interested in marrying him."

"I see. That is most improper of him – a gentleman should adhere to a lady's wishes, even if he fervently hopes for something different. But... your reaction seemed most intense – are you quite certain that there is nothing more to it, to your distress in his presence? I would assist you in any way that I might, if there was need, if you would permit me."

She stilled, and he wondered if he had said too much, had gone well beyond the bounds of propriety himself, in enquiring into her personal state. But the fact that he was quite certain that she lied, that she was keeping secrets from him, when always before, until this last few weeks, she had been refreshingly honest in everything, worried him. She met his gaze, and the soft blue of her eyes was filled with a deep sadness, and something else... fear? Surely not fear of him? Then she turned her head away. Her voice was a little shaky when she spoke.

"Lord Kevin, if there was a way in which you could help me, I would not hesitate to call upon you. But there is nothing you need do for me at this time. I will endure Lord Puglinton's persistent attention, and continue to deny him. I would not create a scandal which might reflect upon my sisters."

He was sure that the words disguised the truth in some way, but he could do nothing but accept them at face value.

"I know that you would not, for you care for them deeply. Even so, should things change, should you need my help..."

"I will ask you. Thank you."

They sat a little longer on the terrace, the heat softened by the light breeze, until they heard the orchestra begin for the next set.

He touched her hand gently, and she rose, nodding. Nothing more was said, and they went inside to dance.

<<<< O >>>>

The following day, Kevin rose late and, after dealing with the day's correspondence, he decided to spend an hour or two at his club. Of late, he had not seen much of the men he had been at school with, and he wondered what was happening in their lives. It was remarkably easy to lose touch, when Chester Park took so much of his time and his thoughts in recent months. Not that he had a lot in common with most of them, but still, connections were worth keeping.

The place was quiet, so early in the day, but a few men were gathered in the lounge, some with coffee, some with brandy. He dropped into a seat beside them, and ordered coffee. Lord Helmwood turned to him, smiling.

"You've been a stranger for a while, Loughbridge – what brings you here today?"

"I've been a stranger, because my sister is about to marry, and my family have been demanding my attention. Today, I am here to escape all of that, and think of other things entirely!"

They laughed sympathetically.

"Perhaps you'd be better with brandy than coffee then!"

Kevin shook his head, and sipped the coffee, which had just been delivered.

"Enough time for brandy later. But tell me – what is new in your lives? So long as it has nothing to do with weddings."

They laughed again, but nodded. Then Helmwood spoke.

"Hmm – well, recently, I've developed a bit of an interest in gossip. Never cared for it before... but now..."

Kevin looked at him, utterly surprised.

"Gossip? Whatever for?"

"It's the 'Gossip Gazette' – have you seen the things they print in that 'Voice of Truth' column? Funnier than any gossip I ever saw or heard before, and remarkably on point for most of it being true. Makes me wonder who the hell writes it, for they certainly have the entrée into society, to be getting so much scandalous information on so many people."

Kevin was intrigued – the more he heard about the scandal sheet the more unusual it seemed.

"Is it really that accurate? I haven't seen the thing, but you're not the first person to mention it to me."

Helmwood reached down beside his chair, and lifted a folded newssheet from the floor. He held it out to Kevin, who took it, curious.

"Here, have a look."

Kevin unfolded it, and located the column, then began to read. The issue in his hands had three articles in the column, and by the time that he was half way through the second one, he wished that he had never begun to read. For the style of the commentary, the flow of the words, was all frighteningly familiar. If he closed his eyes, he could hear Lady Hyacinth's voice, crisp, amused, and scathing, saying exactly these sorts of things, about people they had seen at recent Balls.

Was it possible? Could Lady Hyacinth have written these?

Would she do such a thing, after telling him that her observations were not normally shared with anyone? He could not countenance it, yet the paper in his hand... He swallowed the last of his coffee, and looked up.

"Most interesting, Helmwood. I see what you mean. Might I have this? There is someone I'd like to show it to."

"By all means, old boy, I've read that one all through now. There'll be more where that came from tomorrow."

"My thanks. I'm away now, for I've some business to attend to. Enjoy your day."

Kevin stood, and folded the newssheet carefully, before exiting the club. All the way back to Chester House, his mind tumbled the thought about – if Lady Hyacinth had written these, and deliberately allowed them to be published, then everything he believed about her was made a mockery. He did not wish to accept it. Was not, in fact, willing to accept it, just yet. He could see no option, other than to confront Lady Hyacinth about it. In that moment, he realised just how much he had come to care for her, and how much it mattered to him, that she not have done this in a cold calculated way, lying to him, and everyone else. If she had... then his heart was about to be broken in two.

<<<< O >>>>

The evening was going to be terrible, Hyacinth knew it. For tonight she would tell Lord Puglinton of her decision. She had gone over and over her options in her mind, and had always come back to the same answer. She would refuse to marry him, but would agree to keep writing the gossip articles for him. That, at least, would buy her time, although the thought that her words would be used in such a dreadful way horrified her.

But with time, she could address the other part of the issue. She could find someone else to marry, so that he could never force her to that, in the future. Again, as she thought of it, Lord Kevin came to mind. Oh, how she wished that she could marry him! It would be a delightful solution, one which would not be a hardship. She would still have to hide her writing from him, which would be distressing, but to be saved from ever potentially being forced to marry Lord Puglinton...

She was foolish to even think of it. He had shown no sign of being interested in formally courting her, and she was quite certain that, when he had offered his help, being asked to marry her was not what he would have had in mind!

As they entered the grand parlour of Lady Hepplewood's home, she was thankful, at least, that the evening would not feature dancing. Instead, it was a musical soiree, with a performer who was reputed to be good, but not extraordinary. People milled around, and Hyacinth tried her best to look as if the world was a wonderful place, whilst feeling utterly queasy inside. She made sure that she stayed to the opposite side of the parlour from the door into the room where the performance would occur. When everyone went in, she would have the opportunity, she hoped, to speak quickly to Lord Puglinton, and tell him.

The odious man was there – she had seen him, and he had given her a mocking half bow from a distance. She was sure that, given the chance to speak to her quietly, he would not be able to resist. So far, however, she had not seen Lord Kevin – which left her feeling a little alone and heartsick. She determinedly ignored that feeling, and concentrated on what she needed to do that night. The sooner she had spoken to Puglinton, the better, for at least then she would know what to do next.

After what felt like forever, but was most likely only a half hour or less, a footman announced that guests should start moving into the performance room. People moved forward, clusters of friends hoping to find seats together, all of them talking as they went. None of them looked back. Hyacinth stayed where she was, watching.

As she had half expected, Lord Puglinton moved as if to join the throng, then paused, and looked around. Seeing Hyacinth, he smiled that wolfish smile, and came to her.

"My dear Lady Hyacinth, I am delighted to see you, as always. Have you been writing? I do so hope so. Have you an answer for me? I find myself impatient – perhaps I will not give you as long as I had thought before…."

Hyacinth felt more physically ill than she ever had in her life. She swallowed, hating the words that she was about to say, but reminding herself that she was doing this to protect her sisters' reputations.

"Lord Puglinton. Yes, I have an answer. I will not marry you," his eyes glittered with what she thought was anger, but before he could speak, she went on, "but I will write for you, if that is the price of your silence on this matter. We will need to work out an appropriate method for me to send you packets of the articles."

She was quivering, afraid that he would not accept her words, that he would, after all, attempt to force her to marry him. He stood, glaring at her, and she refused to let herself shake visibly, no matter how much effort it took. His fists clenched at his sides, and Hyacinth almost stepped back from him in fear.

"I am most disappointed, Lady Hyacinth. I thought you more sensible than this. Surely, a comfortable life, as my wife, would be more pleasant than a lonely spinsterhood. And it would certainly make it easier for me to obtain your writing."

His voice was a low threatening growl, and Hyacinth felt the urge to cast up her accounts.

"It is my choice, my Lord."

"I will accept it – for now. I will expect the first new selection of your writing within the week. Do not disappoint me, or perhaps I will cease to be so accommodating."

He gave her a mocking bow, spun on his heel, and went into the performance room, leaving her standing there, alone, staring at the door as it closed behind him. She remained unmoving for a few minutes, until the shaking began to overtake her, then she turned and sought the door to the hallway, the need to escape the room overwhelming.

Blindly, unthinking of anything but reaching the ladies retiring room, in case she did, indeed, cast up her accounts, she rushed into the hallway at some speed. And almost immediately collided with something, someone, very solid. She looked up, panic stricken.

"Lady Hyacinth – whatever is amiss?"

Lord Kevin met her eyes, his full of concern.

"I… I cannot…"

She shook her head, and the shaking intensified. He looked around a moment, then took her hand, drawing her after him into the nearest room, and shutting the door behind them.

It was a study – a simple room, with a desk, some chairs, a couch, and some bookshelves. No candles were lit, and the room was tinted a pale silvery tone by the moonlight which came through the window. A fire burned in the grate, almost down to embers.

In that light he looked almost stern, and his handsome face was cast half in shadow. She shivered, unsure what to do or say. He still held her hand, and he drew her to the couch, encouraging her to sit. She did, for she had no thought of what else to do. She knew now that her instinct had been right – unless she managed to marry another man, and very soon, it was almost a certainty that Lord Puglinton would break the agreement, and force her to marry him.

Lord Kevin's gentle touch on her chin brought her back out of her thoughts. He tilted her face up to him. The warmth of his hand on her skin steadied her.

"Lady Hyacinth, you must tell me what is amiss – for something is obviously very much wrong." She shook her head in denial – she could not tell him, could not tell anyone. He bent towards her, and for a moment, she had the oddest feeling that he meant to kiss her. Then he stilled, as if thinking. His voice when it came was far harsher than she had ever heard from him before. "Lady Hyacinth, is this… distress… something to do with those articles in the 'Gossip Gazette'?"

She froze, swallowing, fear racing through her – how could he know? Frantically, she shook her head in denial, but her expression obviously answered his question. In her already distressed state, she found herself unable to dissemble. Instead, she simply stayed there, waiting for his next words.

"I see. It does indeed relate to that. You wrote those snippets of scandal, didn't you? Were they always intended for publication – did you lie when you said that you did not share such things with others?"

She could not bear it – he thought that she had done all of it on purpose, that she had lied to him! Tears started from her eyes.

"NO! I wrote them, that much is true, but they were never intended to be published, never intended to be seen by anyone but me. I have never lied to you – well, except for saying that I was not distressed, when I was."

<<<< O >>>>

Kevin released the breath that he had not known he was holding. He believed her. The truth of it was written on her face, as much as the truth of her having written them had been. But that still did not explain how her words had come to be published. As he had asked her the question, he had wondered if he was mad – for it was a very big step to go from a worrying suspicion borne of reading the column, to accusing a lady of scandal mongering. But now... now that he knew part of it, he needed to know the rest, and this was most definitely not the place for it.

At any moment, there might be a break in the performance, and anyone might stumble upon them – which would leave them compromised, and forced to marry. The small voice in his mind laughed *'that would not be such a terrible fate'*. The thought gave him pause, but he pushed it away – he did not know if she cared for him... He scanned her face – she had stilled, lips half open, her eyes pleading.

A madness came over him then, and he bent his head to her and brought his lips down on hers. The kiss was hard, full of a longing he had been repressing, yet she did not pull away – on the contrary, she melted against him a little, her lips softening under his. He forced himself to pull back – this was not the time to take advantage of her – no time was! She was in distress and he had... disgust with himself filled him.

"Lady Hyacinth, we must discuss this further – I need to understand what has happened – but this is not the time or the place to talk. At any moment, someone might discover us together, and then we would be compromised, and likely have no choice but to wed."

Her voice was soft, yet the words rang into his mind with great clarity, as they echoed his own previous thought.

"That would not, by any means, be the worst fate."

"I am glad that you view it that way – I would not want you to be utterly horrified by the thought. But enough – I will leave you now, so that you may compose yourself. I will call upon you tomorrow, and we will go for a drive in Hyde Park, where we will be able to speak in some degree of privacy."

He rose, and bowed, his mind in utter turmoil, then turned and left her.

<<<< O >>>>

Hyacinth stared at the closed door, her fingers rising to touch her lips, her heart beating fast.

He had kissed her. And he would call on her tomorrow. Her world had gone mad.

CHAPTER TWELVE

The following day dawned bright and beautiful, yet Hyacinth found herself miserable. She sat in bed, a new journal in her hands, and wrote – hating herself for doing it, yet knowing that she had no choice. She needed to keep Lord Puglinton at least reasonably happy, so that he would not press her further towards marriage. But she would not stop looking for a way to escape his trap completely. The only thing which made the day seem in any way bearable was the prospect of Lord Kevin calling upon her.

Would he come, as he had said he would? She certainly hoped so. The thought of him made her pause, and her fingers rose to her lips again, as she remembered the previous night's kiss. After he had left her in that small study, she had spent some minutes gathering her composure, then slipped out, visited the ladies' retiring room to tidy her appearance, and then gone quietly to sit at the back of the performance room. The performance had been, as expected, nothing exceptional. Blessedly, Puglinton had ignored her for the rest of the evening.

Once her writing for the morning was done, she put the journal away, and rang for Sally. She would dress to suit receiving callers, and believe that he would come. What they might discuss when he did, she did not quite know – for, surely, he would want to know more, and just as surely, she could not tell him. Although she found that she wanted to – wanted the relief of having someone to speak to, of the terrible trap that her carelessness had wrought.

She was, as a consequence, distracted and irritable. Her sisters sighed, and left her alone, expecting that she would recover from whatever had her out of sorts on her own, or would reach a point where she was willing to discuss it with them. By the time that Lord Kevin arrived, she was no closer to a decision on what she might say to him.

Her sisters watched curiously as she greeted him, and the younger girls giggled a little at his cheerful and friendly greetings to them. They sat in the parlour for a short time, before Lord Kevin turned the conversation in the direction that she had been expecting.

"Lady Hyacinth, will you grant me the pleasure of taking you for a drive in Hyde Park, to enjoy this delightful weather?"

Hyacinth swallowed – she wanted to go, yet she knew that he would, inevitably, ask her more about her distress the night before. She could not deny his request without good reason, and, in truth, she did not want to.

"I would be delighted, Lord Kevin. I will call my maid to accompany us."

"I fear that may not be possible – today I am driving the curricle, which has no extra seat."

"Oh."

"Do not be concerned about propriety – it is a very open carriage, and we will be in full public view at all times. I am sure that there is no cause for concern."

Hyacinth thought a moment, then nodded. If she was going to have a conversation with Lord Kevin which even touched on her problems with Lord Puglinton, and her journal, then she did not, really, want Sally to be there to overhear.

"Let us go then. I will just fetch my bonnet."

<<<< O >>>>

Kevin was acutely aware of Lady Hyacinth beside him as they moved through the streets towards Hyde Park. There was a tension in her, as if she was quivering. With fear? Or something else? He did not know. All he knew was that he wanted to reassure her, to help her. Her words of the previous night had echoed in his mind ever since - that being forced to marry him. if compromised, would not be the worst fate – did she really see marrying him as a positive option? Or not? It could be interpreted either way.

Once they reached the Park, he slowed the horses to a walk, and turned to Lady Hyacinth. He saw no way to approach the matter delicately – he would have to rely on her general appreciation for blunt truthfulness.

"Lady Hyacinth – last night… you were most distressed, and you admitted that you had written those gossip pieces, but you stated that they had never been meant to be published. So, I must ask – how did they come to be published? And why were you so very distressed last night? What had occurred?"

She looked at him, and her expression shifted from one emotion to another, at lightning speed. Fear, sadness, hope, confusion, even anger, all seemed to be there momentarily. Then she turned away with a tiny half strangled sob. He damned the fact that he was driving, for he wanted to reach out and hold her.

"I cannot tell you."

"Why? Given that I already know that you wrote them, what can possibly be so much worse, that you cannot tell me? You know by now, I most sincerely hope, that I would never do anything to harm you – I only hope to be able to help in some way."

She lifted her hand to her mouth, as if to hold in the sobs which escaped anyway. He waited, utterly unsure of what might happen, but hoping that she might honour him with her trust. After a few moments, he passed the reins into one hand, and reached out his free hand to gently touch her arm. She made an odd gasping sound, and then spoke, her voice low and shaky.

"I do not know that anyone could help. I am trapped by my own carelessness, and there is no remedy that I can see."

"Nonetheless, will you tell me? Perhaps I will be able to see some possibilities that you cannot."

"I very much doubt that. But… if you can bear to hear of my foolishness, and not castigate me for it, then I believe that I would find it a relief simply to speak of it."

"Lady Hyacinth, I cannot imagine you being foolish – and even if that were the case, I would not condemn you for it – we are all fools at some times in our lives. Please, speak, and unburden your worries upon me."

"I barely know where to begin. Perhaps where it really starts is more than two years ago, when I first came out into society. At that stage, only Lily, Camellia and I were out – then last year two more of my sisters came out and this year, mother gave in to their insistence, and the final two were allowed to come out, even though they are quite young. But when I first came out, I discovered that those of society are not at all forgiving. My family are all most kind and tolerant – I know that I am very lucky in that way. But the *ton* did not take well to my sharpness of tongue, and my tendency to say what I truly thought of things. So I learnt not to say things. But it was so very hard. In the end, I found an old journal that I had not touched since I was a small child, and I began to write my thoughts down in it, each morning after a society event. It somehow relieved the sense of pressure that had been created within me, by the effort of not saying those things directly to people. No one else even knew that the journal existed, but it served its purpose."

"That is, if I may say so, a very wise and clever solution to the problem. For you are right – they are not at all forgiving."

"I came to terms with that. I could not, completely, change who I am – hence my reputation for shrewishness, yet I managed to remain 'barely acceptable'. And things went on that way, until just a few weeks ago. Until that day when you first called upon me. That morning, I had been foolish – I had taken my journal, and my pencil - for carrying ink about is not wise - into the fenced park in the square, to sit in the sun and write. I was there when you arrived. When the footman came to summon me, I hastily pushed the journal out of sight – into my pockets, I thought."

"You thought? So that was not where it actually was?"

"No. But I did not discover that until much later. I rushed back to the house, changed, and came to talk to you. It was only when I returned to my room, after you had departed, that I discovered that the journal was not in my pockets. I was horrified. I searched everywhere – in my room, in the house, on the way to the park, and in the park – but it was gone. I was frightened – what if someone found it? But at least it did not have my name written in it anywhere – there was only a very blotchy attempt at a watercolour of a hyacinth, which I had done as a small child. Then, in the park, near the bench where I had been sitting, I found my pencil – but not the journal. The only conclusion I could make, was that someone had found the journal, and taken it. I was very afraid that whoever had found it might, somehow, work out that I had written it, and might condemn me amongst society for it. But what happened was far worse than just that."

"Worse? Because your writings were published? But… do you know who found it, who has done this?"

"I did not at first, but I do now."

"Then tell me, please – surely there is a way that we can stop them?"

She gave a bitter laugh, and shook her head.

"It is not so simple. I did not know that my words had been published, until you spoke to me of the 'Gossip Gazette'. I had the worst feeling about it, so I obtained a copy. And yes, they were my words. At that point, I had no idea who had done this, but I was horrified all over again. What if someone worked it out, if they remembered that I had been present on all of those occasions?"

"But why would they think it was you?"

"For the same reason that you did. Because of my sharp tongue, and my reputation for that. They would think 'who would say such things, this way' and I would be a likely person to come to mind. So I spent many days simply terrified – I stopped speaking to people at social events, unless I absolutely had to. I resolved to never write my thoughts down again. Then, a few weeks ago, as we were all caught up in Lily's wedding preparations, I discovered who it was who had done this – in the worst possible way."

"Who is it? And how did they reveal themselves? What do they stand to gain from doing this?"

"What do they stand to gain? At a minimum, profit. But what they had hoped to gain was me, as both a wife, and a permanent source of gossip writing."

Kevin was silent, staring at her in shock – *'as a wife'*? Was that the *'worst fate'* that she had referred to, when saying that marrying him would not be the worst fate?

"Who?"

It was almost a demand – he could hear the anger in his own voice.

"Lord Puglinton. He has taken a house across the square from ours, for the Season. He must have walked in the park, and found it. And it seems that he is at least a major investor in that dreadful paper. Somehow, he worked out that it was me. He threatened me – gave me an ultimatum. I had a few weeks to choose – either marry him, and keep writing for him, or not marry him, but still keep writing for him, or refuse, and be revealed to society, and have my sisters' reputations ruined."

"The cad!"

"I would, perhaps, use worse words than that, if ladies were permitted to swear. He seemed to think that, of course I would marry him, for he believes that no fate could be worse than living life as a spinster. But I told him quite clearly that, whilst I would continue to write for him, because I saw no other way to protect my sisters, I would not marry him. I told him that last night. And he laughed, and said that he 'would accept that for now, but that I had best do exactly as he wanted, or he might rethink his generosity, and require marriage as the price of his ongoing silence'. That was what sent me fleeing towards the ladies' retiring room, once he had walked away from me. For I cannot but imagine that he will choose to do that, sooner rather than later, so that he can have my dowry, and my person, as well as my words. The very idea revolts me to my core. But I can see no way to escape this trap. The only idea that I have had, which might at least prevent him from forcing me to marry him, is the fact that such a thing would be impossible, if I were already married to someone else. But that would not stop him from forcing me to write for him."

Kevin sat, the sun warm on his face, the horses walking quietly along through the Park, the day perfect around them, and allowed her words to sink in. She was right – he could see no other immediate way to lessen the risk to her, nor could he see a way to remove the threat entirely – but he was resolved to find one. *'If I was already married to someone else'* – suddenly, the very idea of Lady Hyacinth married to anyone else seemed utterly abhorrent. He had to save her – but could he...?

"That is, truly, a terrible situation in which you find yourself. But there must be a way out. There must be!"

"If there is, I do not know what it may be."

"Neither do I, right at this moment. But I will think upon it, and I will not rest until I discover a solution for you."

"I thank you for your care for me – although I do not think that there is a solution to find. I am trapped in this situation by my own foolish carelessness, and I must live with the consequences."

Kevin looked at her, filled with an intense desire to hold her close, to kiss her, to somehow, magically, make the difficult situation disappear. But he could not. They drove on, the day perfect around them, but neither of them in a state of mind to appreciate it. Something, however, niggled in Kevin's mind, about the whole thing. There was something about the 'Gossip Gazette' some piece of information that he had heard, which now seemed important to him, but which he could not immediately recall. He would worry at that until he did recall it. But for now, all he could do was return her to her home, and hope that Puglinton did not become totally unreasonable, too soon. For he needed to go back to Chester Park the following day, as Charles and Maria's wedding day loomed close.

<<<< O >>>>

Hyacinth did feel somewhat better for having spoken of it all, yet it was clear that Lord Kevin agreed with her analysis – there was, at least at present, nothing to be done, but for her to keep writing for Lord Puglinton. Lord Kevin had paused for a long time, immediately after she had admitted to her idea of marrying someone else to protect her form being forced to marry Lord Puglinton. Had he realised that, in her mind, and, if she was honest, her heart, she wished that person to be him?

125

She was not sure if she wished that he had, or he had not. The days loomed ahead of her, depressingly threatening, but the fact that someone else now knew of her plight had made it, just a little, easier to bear.

<<<< O >>>>

As the carriage took him to Chester Park yet again, Kevin worried about leaving Lady Hyacinth – not that his presence could, in any way directly reduce her troubles, but still, it felt like abandoning her. Eventually, he slipped into a half-doze, lulled by the steady rocking of the carriage. Thoughts flitted through his mind, almost dream like.

Then, as if finally choosing to answer the question he had been asking himself since the conversation in the Park, with Lady Hyacinth, a memory surfaced. He snapped awake. There had been that conversation with his father, some time ago, where they had mentioned the 'Gossip Gazette' – what had his father said?

'There was some bad business with that one, a year or so ago, if I remember aright. It used to be more of a respectable newssheet, but the man who owned most of it ran into trouble, with gambling, or some such, and the 'Commentator' changed hands. I assumed that it had been used to pay off a debt. But there were rumours – which suggested that the card games involved had been rigged in some way, that the man had been set up to lose. He lost everything, and left the country to escape his other debtors. Very bad business that. But no one ever proved anything, that I know of, and the new owner has made it much more of a scurrilous scandal sheet than anything else.'

And if Lord Puglinton was now the primary owner of the 'Society Commentator' – commonly known as 'The Gossip Gazette', then that would make him the man who had won it, from the previous owner, in a potentially rigged game of cards. Given the man's blackmail of Lady Hyacinth, Kevin had no difficulty believing him capable of intentionally ruining a man, so that he might get his hands on the man's assets.

And if that was true...

Then, with a little digging by Kevin's friends, many of whom had been, or were, spies for the Crown, then evidence to that effect might be uncovered.

Kevin contemplated that for a while, as the countryside rolled past outside the window. The question was – if he could obtain such evidence, what would he do with it?

The immediate, most logical thought, was to blackmail the blackmailer. The very idea made him feel dirty, yet... what better way to free Lady Hyacinth from the trap in which she found herself?

For, if Puglinton had done such a thing once, it was quite likely that he had done it a number of times – and depending on the exact circumstances, he may well have been considerably beyond the law in doing so. If evidence of such was revealed, Puglinton might lose everything, not simply society's approval. It was tempting, very tempting.

Kevin held the idea carefully in mind. He would set things in motion through his friends, and also question his father further – perhaps his father already knew enough to allow them to know where to look for more evidence. And, there was one other thing which he could do...

He could marry Lady Hyacinth, if she would have him.

For having to leave her, now, when she was so distressed, and so alone, had made him realise just how much he wanted to be with her – made him realise that, somewhere in the last few months, he had come to love her.

Even if nothing came of his investigation into Puglinton, marrying her would at least in part protect her.

But... could he convince her that he wanted to marry her, because he loved her? For he was quite certain that she would immediately assume that he was 'sacrificing himself' and doing the noble thing to protect her. He would need a way to convince her that his personal wishes, and that need, coincided.

CHAPTER THIRTEEN

Charles and Maria's wedding was done, and they had departed for the north. Now, two days later, Kevin sat with his father again – it was time to ask the questions about the 'Gossip Gazette' and Lord Puglinton. Watching Charles and Maria together had made Kevin even more certain that he wanted that sort of happiness with Lady Hyacinth – and that he wanted to be back in London, as soon as possible.

"Do you remember, Father, what we spoke of, when I was here a month or so ago? About the bad business you knew of, that had gone on with the 'Society Commentator'? I am interested to know more of it, for it seems that the whole mess has affected some friends of mine."

"Oh, that's not a good thing. I hope they weren't taken in by that card shark – didn't lose anything major, did they?"

"No, nothing too bad, fortunately. But you implied that everyone thought that cheating was involved? Who was it – you never did mention a name?"

"Didn't I? Well, I don't like to malign a man when it was never proven, but still, it seemed entirely too neat not to be true. It was Puglinton. Spent a year or so playing cards hard after his wife died. Always seemed to win – and always from men who had property or business assets. He oh so kindly accepted those assets in payment of the debts. Not long after he got his hands on the paper, he just stopped playing."

"How many of the *ton* know about this? It seems the sort of thing that would get around."

"Not many. He was mostly careful, but a few of us knew – friend of mine understands how to cheat at cards, even if he doesn't – and he watched Puglinton a few times, and told me never to play with the man, for he was sure that he cheated."

"I see. Are you willing to put me in contact with that friend?"

"Certainly. I'll write down the name and direction for you, before you go back to London."

"Thank you. Now, on a completely different topic – now that Charles and Maria are wed, and off on their wedding trip, will you do as you promised and see a physician? You look paler and more worn every time that I see you."

His father looked away, fidgeting with his brandy glass, then looked back with a sigh.

"Yes, alright. It is time, although I warn you, there will be nothing he can do."

"I will wait to hear his opinion, before I believe that."

"Well and good, I'll send a letter, asking him to come."

The June sun was hot, and London's streets were beginning to have a very distinct aroma, at least in the poorer districts. Yet the sun felt good on Kevin's face as he drove his curricle towards Elbury House. He had spent the day before yesterday visiting his sister, Nerissa, the Duchess of Melton, and speaking quietly with her husband about the information he sought, on Lord Puglinton's less than savoury past with gambling. Hunter had been a spy for the Crown during the war, and still had all of the required contacts. For all that Kevin knew, he might still be on call by the Crown. Kevin did not ask – he simply accepted Hunter's word that investigation would happen, and quickly.

He had, yet again, been left almost jealous by observing others' happiness. Nerissa was expecting, and had been stubbornly still attending society events, seeing no reason to hide away from the world. She hoped, she said, to start a new fashion for enceinte women still socialising. He had to admire her courage.

This morning, a messenger had come to Chester House, with a note from Hunter. All it said was 'there is evidence, and a witness'. It was all that Kevin needed to put his plan into action. He had not gone to Lady Hyacinth since returning to London, no matter how much he had wanted to - for he had wanted to have something to give her hope, before speaking to her. Now, he was more than eager to see her.

When he drew up before Elbury House, the usual footman came down to take his horses heads.

"Will you be long, my Lord? Should I take them around to the mews?"

Kevin smiled at the man.

"No, thank you – I hope to be taking Lady Hyacinth for a drive shortly. If that is not possible, I will send someone out to let you know."

"Very good, my Lord."

Kevin almost bounced up the steps, so eager was he to see her, and Marks, the butler, could not repress his smile at the enthusiasm as he opened the door.

"Good day, Lord Kevin. The young ladies are in the green parlour – shall I show you through?"

"Yes, thank you, Marks. I trust that Lady Hyacinth is with her sisters?"

"Yes, my Lord."

The butler closed the door after him, and led him through the house, then announced him at the parlour door. The conversation in the room stopped, and six sets of eyes focussed on him. Suddenly, he felt a little overwhelmed – what did her sisters think of him? Would they approve, if – no, when – he asked her to marry him? Lady Hyacinth came forward, and suddenly, he no longer cared what the others thought.

She was beautiful, as always, but her face showed the strain – she looked tired, and almost nervous – an expression that he had never seen on her face before.

"Lord Kevin! It is good to see you. I had wondered if you had abandoned London for the summer, already."

"Most definitely not. I was, however called away on family matters. Might I persuade you to allow me to take you for a drive, now that I am back?"

Her eyes lit up with pleasure at his words, and it transformed her face for a moment – this was the Lady Hyacinth that he knew!

"I would be delighted. Just let me fetch a bonnet."

He bowed, and she sped past him, and up the stairs. He turned back to the room, to find the others studying him curiously. Camellia came forward, and spoke very quietly.

"She has not been happy, these last few weeks. Yet she smiled for you just now. I hope that you can make her keep smiling."

Kevin met Camellia's eyes, and nodded.

"So do I, very much."

"Good."

Camellia went back to her sisters, and they all went back to their previous conversation, leaving Kevin standing there, feeling a little lost. He stepped back out into the hallway to wait for Lady Hyacinth. He did not have to wait for long – she was soon standing before him, a very fetching bonnet tied over her hair. He offered her his arm, and led her out to the curricle.

Once again, they were silent until they reached the Park, where he could slow to a very sedate walk, and give her his attention. Suddenly, he was not entirely sure where to start – he had so much to say, and so much to ask of her – a thread of fear knotted his stomach – what if she did not, in the end, care enough for him to consider his proposal? He pushed it aside – this was no time for cowardice. He reminded himself, mentally, of everything that he needed to say, then took a deep breath and began.

"Lady Hyacinth, I must first apologise for having been away so long, leaving you with no idea of where I was, or what I was doing. I have much to tell you, and much to explain. Last time we spoke, you gifted me your trust, and told me of your terrible predicament. I hope that nothing has worsened in that matter, while I have been away?"

"No, nothing has changed. I write each morning, after any social event, then I copy those writings out, and send them, via a street urchin, to the address provided by Lord Puglinton. He has not, as yet, pressed for anything more – but I do not, in any way, trust him to stay so forbearing. And every time I hear someone mention the 'Gossip Gazette', or I see a copy with my words on the page, I die a little inside."

Kevin reached out and took her hand in his, squeezing her fingers firmly. She met his eyes, and smiled – it was a faded smile, still full of unhappiness, yet it filled him with warmth.

"I am glad that things are not worse. But let me tell you where I have been, and why. This past few days, I have been back in London, pursuing an investigation which began as a result of a conversation with my father. Before that, I was at Chester Park, with my family – as I have been each time that I have left London during this Season. This last visit was for a joyous occasion – the marriage of my sister, Maria, to a good man. After the disaster that was her first marriage, which left her a miserable widow, this is wonderful indeed. But it was also a visit which contained much concern on my part, as has every visit I have made there this year. For you see, my father is ill – quite seriously, and has been hiding it from the rest of the family. He would not allow me to reveal it, nor would he see a physician, until Maria was wed."

"Oh dear – that sounds most worrying – what manner of illness is it?"

"I do not yet truly know – it involves his lungs, and causes him to sometimes cough up blood. He has lost weight, and has less energy. Perhaps worst of all, he himself believes it to be terminal – he tells me that his grandfather suffered something similar, and was dead within the year. I struggle to accept it with the equanimity that he does. Especially as I could do nothing about it, nor could I speak of it to anyone. At least now that Maria is wed, he has agreed to call in the physician. But there was more to my visit this time, as well. As I mentioned, a conversation with my father resulted in me coming back to London to arrange a very specific investigation. You see, on my way to Chester Park, I remembered something that my father had said, one previous visit. I had, that time, mentioned the fact that the *ton* were all agog at the new column in the 'Gossip Gazette', and he had commented on the history of the newssheet. I had forgotten his words, until well after you had honoured me by telling me of your troubles."

"And what did he say? How is it relevant to my problems, if it is at all?"

"It is most relevant to your problems, for I believe that it holds the solution to them."

She gasped, regarding him wide-eyed.

"A solution? To everything? I cannot credit that it is possible."

"It is definitely possible, although I must say that I am not enamoured of the means required."

"The means required?"

"Yes. What my father told me was that the current owner of the 'Gossip Gazette' had obtained it as payment of a gambling debt – a debt, which it was believed by my father and some friends of his, had been created as a result of a card game in which the winner had cheated. They believed that the man in question had obtained quite a few business and property assets that way – by cheating, ruining good men, then 'generously' accepting those assets as payment of the debts. My father confirmed that the man in question was Lord Puglinton."

"I see. I am not surprised – I believe that he is capable of almost any underhanded dealings. But how does knowing this help me?"

"Well... I had an idea, and I did not want to tell you, until I had confirmed that it might work. When I got back to London, I went to visit my other sister – Nerissa. And I spoke at length with her husband, who still has many... contacts... with access to resources and information that most do not have."

"I understand what you mean."

"Good. I asked him to see if there was evidence obtainable, of Puglinton's misdeeds. He found it. Evidence, and, apparently, a witness. With that, I am confident that we can free you from Puglinton."

"But how? I don't understand."

"By blackmailing the blackmailer. Unpleasant as it is, that seems the only option. If he wants to keep his assets, and his place in society, he will not want any of this revealed. And releasing you, returning your journal, and ceasing to publish the 'Voice of Truth' column, will seem a small price to him."

She was silent, deeply thoughtful, Unconsciously, she drew her lip between her teeth a little as she thought. He wanted to kiss her.

"I am not at all sure that I approve, in principle. But I am quite certain that I approve, in practice, if it frees me from him completely. But... I must ask... why? Why have you done this for me?"

"Why have I done this for you? Because, Lady Hyacinth Gardenbrook, I love you. I think that I have done so for quite some time, but this last week has made me aware of just how important you are to me. I cannot imagine my life without you. I... I want to marry you, Hyacinth."

Her blue eyes widened, and her lips formed a little 'O' for a moment.

"You... you love me? You want to marry me? You're not just..."

"No, I am not just 'being noble, and offering myself as a way of ensuring that you are safe from Puglinton'. I love you. I want to marry you, because of who you are, regardless of Puglinton or anything else. Can you... can you possibly consider it? Can you come to care for me?"

She laughed then, with a slight edge of hysteria to it. But she reached for his hand.

"Can I come to care for you? I already do care for you. I think that I began loving you that very first night we were introduced, when you did not turn away from my sharp tongue, no matter how much I intentionally challenged you! I was just afraid that you did not feel the same, that when you disappeared..."

"Oh! You feared, perhaps, that I had a mistress somewhere?" She nodded, blushing. It was Kevin's turn to laugh. "No, there isn't, and never has been, a mistress. I am not prone to flattery enough to keep one happy – and such women do not like bluntness at all!"

Unable to resist any longer, he leant to her, and gently brought his lips to hers – it was barely a brush, yet it sent heat flooding through his veins. When he drew back, she was blushing. They both completely ignored the fact that they were in a public place, that anyone might have seen.

"I think that I would be most happy for you to blackmail Puglinton. I find myself feeling vengeful."

"Then I shall put that plan into action. But, let me do this formally, for I would hear your answer directly. Lady Hyacinth Gardenbrook, will you marry me?"

"I will, and gladly – just as soon as I know that I am truly free of Lord Puglinton."

"It shall be done. And now... I should, really, do the officially correct thing, and speak to your father."

"Yes, but I do not think that you have anything to fear there – after all, you like talking about agriculture with him!"

Kevin laughed, and turned the curricle back towards Elbury House.

CHAPTER FOURTEEN

As they came to a halt before Elbury House, Kevin felt a moment of complete fear – what if the Duke disapproved? He chastised himself for doubting – after all, Lady Hyacinth's observation was correct – he did enjoy discussing agriculture with the Duke, and he was almost certain that the man approved of him. Still, he felt nervous as they entered the house.

"Marks, is my father in his study?"

"Yes, my Lady."

Marks watched as Lady Hyacinth led Kevin to the door of the Duke's study, but said nothing more.

Lady Hyacinth rose on her toes, and pressed a delicate kiss to Kevin's cheek, before backing away.

"I'll be in the parlour, once you've…"

Kevin nodded, and tapped on the door.

"Enter."

Kevin went in, shutting the door behind him. The Duke rose from his desk, a curious expression on his face.

"Lord Kevin – what can I do for you today? For I presume that you are here for something other than a brandy and a chat about farming and the cultivation of exotic flowers?"

Kevin swallowed, and nodded.

"Yes, Your Grace. I… I am here to speak to you about your daughter – about Lady Hyacinth."

"Oh-ho! So that's the way it is, eh? Well then, take a seat, my boy."

The Duke waved towards the two chairs set either side of the fireplace, and Kevin obediently went to them, and sat. The Duke dropped into the other chair, and regarded him, waiting.

"Your Grace… I… I wish to marry Lady Hyacinth. I… I hope that you might see your way clear to approve my suit."

The Duke was completely still for a moment, regarding Kevin, and the tick of the clock on the mantel seemed to echo in the room. After a moment, the Duke gave an emphatic nod, then rose, and Kevin watched him, suddenly afraid that he would, after all, be rejected. But the Duke simply went to the sideboard which was set against the wall, pulled the stopper from the brandy decanter that sat there, and poured two glasses.

"It looks like we'll need that brandy after all – to toast your future happiness."

He carried the glasses back, and handed one to Kevin.

Kevin released his breath in a rush, and his hand shook slightly as he took the glass.

"Then... then you approve, Your Grace?"

"I do. Most heartily. I'm grateful, in fact, my boy – Hyacinth has always been the one I've worried about. She's a strong mind, strong character, but she has struggled so hard to be 'socially acceptable'. I was beginning to wonder if there was a man out there who had enough character to match her. I assume... that you've already spoken to her, that she's happy with this? I'd not, ever, force any of them to a match they didn't want."

"I have, Your Grace, just this afternoon. And I have been honoured by her acceptance of my proposal."

"Excellent. You'll do well by her, I think."

"You... you are not concerned that I will only be a Viscount, in the fullness of time? You did not hope for a man of higher station for her?"

"Frankly, Lord Kevin, I do not care what station a man holds, if he is the man that my daughter wants, and is well off enough to support her appropriately. Her happiness is far more important than the title she will carry. And a man's competence is far more important than the title he holds, or will hold. I realise that those statements would shock most of the *ton* to the core, but they are my opinions, and I'll stick by them."

"I am most glad that you see the world that way. It took my sister, Maria, suffering for a year with a terrible man, and then suffering more when he met an unpleasant death, to teach my father to think that way."

The Duke nodded, and sipped his brandy.

"Just make her happy, Lord Kevin. And if your fortunes ever suffer, apply to me for aid – I'd not have my daughter want for anything, should you have a temporary reversal of fortune."

"Thank you, Your Grace. I believe that you can rest easy on that count. The Chester estates are profitable, and well managed, and I've learnt enough from my father, and, I must admit, from my neighbours, to keep them that way."

"Good to hear, good to hear. Well then – I've no doubt that she's in the parlour, waiting anxiously for the moment that she can tell her sisters. You are prepared for the immediate chaos that will ensue, aren't you?"

"I believe that I am…"

"Then, by all means, go and set my household into turmoil again. The Duchess will be in alt about having another wedding to plan."

Kevin swallowed the last of his brandy, rose, bowed to the Duke, and left the room.

<<<< O >>>>

Hyacinth had entered the parlour quietly, and simply settled onto the couch beside Rose, saying nothing. The conversation in the room, which was about the rather daring gown that Miss Phillibert had worn the previous evening, continued. Rose raised an eyebrow at her silence, and passed her the plate of little iced cakes which sat beside her. Hyacinth took it, and selected a cake. If nothing else, it was an excuse not to speak.

The cake was delicious, as always. Cook was a genius.

And Rose probably had some influence on that. Hyacinth had no idea why Rose found such things interesting, but she spent as much time talking to Cook about cakes as their father spent talking to the gardener about flowers.

The sisters had almost managed to reach agreement on Miss Phillibert's dress when the door opened. Hyacinth managed not to choke on the last crumbs of her cake. Lord Kevin stood there, his eyes alight, and she felt a shiver of relief run through her. Not that she had ever thought that her father might deny them... but still. He stepped into the room, and her sisters fell silent, regarding him with wide eyes. He said nothing, but held out his hand to Hyacinth. She rose, and went to him.

Once she faced her sisters beside him, her hand securely in his, he spoke.

"Ladies, your sister has done me the honour of agreeing to become my wife. I have been assured by both Lady Hyacinth, and by your father, that this announcement will result in a situation where the entire world becomes focussed on wedding planning."

The sisters looked at each other, and burst into laughter, then rushed forward to congratulate them. Violet slipped out into the hall, and spoke to Marks for a moment. Not long after, the Duchess swept into the room.

"What is this that I hear? Another wedding?" When Hyacinth nodded, her mother smiled widely. "Wonderful, wonderful. Is you mother in town at present, Lord Kevin? I must meet her to discuss this, as soon as possible!"

"She is not – she is at Chester Park, still. My father... has not been entirely well."

"Then we shall have to visit Chester Park, in the very near future. But there are many things that I can set in motion here, first."

Hyacinth thought that Lord Kevin withstood it all remarkably well – her family were rather like a torrent in flood – they tended to sweep people along with their enthusiasm. The rest of the day passed in happy chaos – her only concern was the fact that Lord Puglinton's threats still loomed over her. Until Lord Kevin carried out his plan, she would not feel entirely safe, ever. And after that... it would depend on how well that plan worked.

<<<< O >>>>

Kevin tucked the satchel of documents under his arm. It was an unassuming thing, much like the ones that men of business carried to transport their papers. But this one contained documents which could ruin a man, and set a lady free. Behind him, Hunter Barrington, the Duke of Melton, stepped down from the carriage, and told the coachman to wait nearby.

When Kevin had gone back to Hunter to discuss his plan for dealing with Lord Puglinton and to collect whatever documents Hunter's contacts had gathered, he had been surprised, and pleased, when his brother-in-law had insisted on accompanying him. For his rank as a Duke would lend weight to the matter, and Kevin was sure that Puglinton, like a large percentage of the *ton*, was aware of the fact that Hunter's responsibilities, during the war, were rumoured to have involved spying. He was not a man that anyone would wish as an enemy, if they were wise.

"Are you ready for this, Kevin? I expect that he will bluster and try to deny everything."

"Of course he will. Until he realises that the threat is serious."

"True – hopefully, once he does, he will take the sensible course of action, and co-operate."

They went up the steps, and rapped the knocker on the door. Soon, they heard the echo of footsteps approaching, inside the house. The door opened, and an elderly butler regarded them.

"How may I help you, gentlemen?"

"We are here to see Lord Puglinton, on an urgent matter."

Kevin passed his, and Hunter's, calling cards to the butler, whose eyebrows rose a little as he read the name of the rather exalted gentleman on his doorstep.

"Please, come in." They entered, and he showed them into a pleasant parlour, with a large window which overlooked the street. "I will inform his lordship of your presence."

They waited, studying the room around them. It reflected wealth, without excessive opulence, although the colour scheme was less than tasteful. Ten minutes passed and, just as they began to wonder if Lord Puglinton would actually deign to see them, he appeared at the parlour door.

"Your Grace, Lord Kevin – to what do I owe this visit?"

"Please shut the door, Puglinton – we have a serious, and private, matter to discuss with you."

Hunter's voice was cold. Lord Puglinton frowned, unaccustomed to being directed in his own home, but complied.

"A serious matter?"

"Yes. A matter upon which might hinge your fortune, and your place in society."

Puglinton's eyes widened in shock, and it was obvious that he was mentally cataloguing all of the things in his life which might put such things at risk. When Kevin and Hunter had discussed how they would approach this, they had planned their words most carefully. They wanted Puglinton off-balance from the start. It appeared to be working.

"What on earth are you talking about?"

There was an edge of bluster to Puglinton's words, which seemed to cover true worry. Kevin spoke, watching Puglinton's reaction to every word.

"Let me be blunt, Lord Puglinton. I have become aware of the fact that a very large number of your assets have been… obtained… as payment of gambling debts. A most unusual number. Debts which were incurred by gentlemen in a series of games, at a well-known gaming hell, over a two-year period. A period during which you cheated, consistently."

Puglinton went red in the face, and drew himself up.

"What nonsense! You have no proof for this scurrilous accusation!"

"On the contrary, Lord Puglinton, proof is exactly what we do have. We have come into possession of a collection of correspondence, in which you were foolish enough to actually plan these matters with an accomplice. An accomplice who has seen his way to cooperate with us, given that you never paid him the entirety of what you had promised. We also have a second witness, who observed each one of those games."

At Kevin's words, Puglinton had gone very pale, all of the previous flush draining from his face. He made one more attempt at bluster, however.

"What ludicrous accusations! I deny all of it."

"Then you are a fool. If we reveal these documents, and the sworn witness statements, to the magistrates and to society, you will not only be ostracised, but will most likely be charged with a number of crimes. As gentlemen, we wanted to give you the opportunity to avoid such disgrace. But obviously, we have wasted our time."

"Now, now, don't be too hasty. If I accept, for a single moment, the idea that these 'proofs' do exist, what do you gentlemen stand to gain, by speaking with me now, rather than simply exposing it all? I must assume that there would be a price for your forbearance."

"How astute of you, Lord Puglinton. Yes, there would be a price, for allowing you to continue to live as you have – with wealth and social position."

"How much? I can be as blunt as you can, gentlemen."

"The price is not one which will be paid in money, Lord Puglinton, not directly. There are four conditions on which we will leave your sins unexposed. One – you will never gamble again. Two – you will cease to print the 'Voice of Truth' column in the 'Society Commentator', three – you will hand to me now, the red leather covered journal which rightfully belongs to Lady Hyacinth Gardenbrook, and four, you will never attempt to threaten Lady Hyacinth again, in any way, on any matter. You may not do any more than greet her politely at social events."

Puglinton blustered again, pacing about the room.

"Never gamble! Preposterous! And what journal? Really, these are most peculiar conditions."

"Nonetheless, they are the only conditions on which your reputation may be saved. I know that you have the journal, and you would be wise to admit it, and comply. Otherwise, your misdemeanours will be well-known within days."

"How do I know that you really have what you say you have?"

Kevin opened the satchel, and drew forth a stack of papers. Selecting one, he handed the rest to Hunter, and took that one to Puglinton, holding it up that Puglinton might see it. The man's eyes trailed over the page for a moment, then he raised his gaze to meet Kevin's. He slumped where he stood, and his defeat was clear in his expression.

"I see."

"Yes, we have the entire correspondence, which makes your guilt very clear."

"Very well then. You have my agreement. What you ask is, in the end, a small price to pay for my reputation and my business interests. Please, come with me."

They followed him down the hall, and into a well-appointed study, where Puglinton unlocked a drawer in his desk, and withdrew a dark red leather-bound book. Kevin took it, and opened it, confirming that it genuinely was Lady Hyacinth's journal. He nodded, satisfied.

"Thank you. You have made a wise decision."

Puglinton looked as if he wished to spit in their faces.

"Now that you have what you came for, get out!"

"I am happy to leave. But... remember – we are watching you, we have excellent contacts, and if you do not comply with the agreement we have made, your misdemeanours will be immediately exposed. I expect to see a notice in tomorrow's 'Society Commentator', announcing that the 'Voice of Truth' column has been permanently discontinued. It has *not* been a pleasure doing business with you, in any way. Good day, Lord Puglinton."

They turned and left, without any further acknowledgement of the man's existence. The old butler regarded them with some confusion, but opened the door as requested. He slammed it after them.

They walked along the street to where the carriage waited.

"Thank you for your assistance. I fear that he would not have been anywhere near so easily convinced without your status as a Duke, and your reputation as having spies as connections, backing me."

"What use is it, to be a Duke, if I cannot use it to assist my friends at times? Something must balance out the endless social obligations and the huge estates to manage!" Kevin handed Hunter the satchel of papers, keeping Lady Hyacinth's journal in his grasp. Hunter smiled as he took them. "I will lock these away in a suitable place – a place from which the right people can easily retrieve them, should Lord Puglinton renege on his promises."

"Thank you, again."

Hunter stepped up into the carriage, and rapped for the coachman to drive on. Kevin turned, the journal tucked under his arm, and walked around the square towards Elbury House.

CHAPTER FIFTEEN

Hyacinth had just finished writing in her new journal, hating the fact that Lord Puglinton would publish her words, but afraid to do anything other than what he had requested, until she knew what had happened. For Lord Kevin had assured her that, within this few days, his plan would be put into action. She rang for Sally, then stared out of the window at the perfect early summer day as Sally fastened the buttons at the back of her gown.

Her mind was a tangle of conflicting emotion – that Lord Kevin loved her, that they would marry, still seemed impossibly wonderful, yet the spectre of Lord Puglinton's threats still hung over her. Once Sally had fastened the last button, and set the last pin in her hair, Hyacinth left her room, intending to go to the parlour, where her sisters were, no doubt, engaged in vigorous debate over some inconsequential thing. But before she reached the stairs, she found Marks hurrying towards her.

"My Lady! Lord Kevin is here, and asks that you see him privately."

Hyacinth's heart pounded wildly. Why would he want privacy, unless it was to give her news of the success, or failure of his plan?

"Thank you, Marks. Where…?"

"I have shown him into the library, my Lady."

Hyacinth nodded, and set off towards the library, her heart still pounding. What would he tell her?

The library door was ajar, and she wasted no time in entering, and closing it behind her. He stood near the window, gazing out at the garden. As always, the sight of him quite took her breath away.

At the sound of the door, he turned towards her, a broad smile on his face. He said nothing, but instead extended his arms towards her, palms flat. On those palms rested the familiar red leather-bound journal. Relief coursed through her, and she wavered, grasping the edge of a nearby bookcase for support.

"My journal… does this mean…?"

"Yes. Our plan has been successful. The man is, at the core, a coward. When his reputation and his fortune were threatened, he very rapidly ceased to bluster, and agreed to our terms. It is often so with those who threaten others – they have no courage of their own. But come, take your journal."

She drew herself up, steadied by his words, and went to him, lifting the journal from his hands. She looked at it, opened it, and assured herself that all of the pages were still intact, then she set it aside, on the small escritoire which stood by the window, and turned back to Lord Kevin.

"Thank you."

She stepped forward then, her face lifted to his, and he reached out, and drew her into his arms. His lips came down upon hers, and she melted into the kiss, a mad and reckless sense of joy filling her. She was safe! He had saved her. And he loved her! The kiss deepened, full of the promise of passion to come, and her lips parted on a sigh of pleasure, as his tongue traced their outline. Heat flooded her body, and the world seemed to fade away, until there was only the sensation of his lips on hers, his arms around her.

Eventually, they drew apart, their breathing uneven, their eyes shining.

"Tomorrow, in the 'Gossip Gazette', you will see a statement which sadly discontinues the 'Voice of Truth' column. Lord Puglinton will never approach you again, beyond a normal polite greeting as is required at social occasions. Nor will he ever gamble again – for we could not allow him to ruin others for his own gain, by cheating, again."

"That is wonderful to hear!" She turned, and lifted the journal. "I had best take this, and put it safely away, immediately. I will see you in the parlour shortly. For, whilst we are betrothed, I should not spend too much time alone with you here… it could still be seen as rather scandalous…"

He bowed, with a soft laugh, and waved her to the door.

<<<< O >>>>

Kevin had received a letter from his mother. In it, she spoke of his father's failing health, and her deepening concern. She asked that Kevin return to Chester Park, as soon as possible. She did not, explicitly, say that she feared that Lord Chester was dying, but the unwritten words were still clear to Kevin.

He sent a letter in return, assuring her that he would be there soon, but also that he would be bringing guests, as a result of his having become betrothed to Lady Hyacinth Gardenbrook. He hoped that the news would bring his mother joy, in the midst of her distress about his father.

Over the next two days, as preparations for the trip to Chester Park proceeded, Kevin's mind came back to his mother's letter, over and over, and to his father's words, some months ago – *'I don't know how long I have, but I doubt it's more than a year, at most'*. What if his father was right? What if he was dying? Was that, truly, why he had been so glad to see Maria married again? Was that why he had urged Kevin to marry?

What if... what if his father did not live long enough to see him married to Lady Hyacinth? The thought horrified him. He wanted his father at his wedding. He sat, pondering, then leapt up. He would, this very moment, go and obtain a marriage license. A common license should be enough, for they could marry in the small church near Chester Park – what was important was to remove the need to wait whilst the banns were read – what if his father did not have the weeks that would take?

All else was in readiness, he believed, for the Duke of Elbury, and his family, to depart for Chester Park the following morning. Kevin himself was packed and ready. So the license was all that was needed. He called for his coat and hat, and hurried to the door.

<<<< O >>>>

Kevin looked at his father, and knew that his fears were true.

Lord Chester had greeted them cheerfully, overjoyed at the news of Kevin's betrothal, and had maintained that positive attitude throughout dinner, and beyond. Now that their guests had retired for the night, Kevin sat with his father, alone in the study, a brandy in his hand. Lord Chester's face was grey, and he coughed often, no longer able to repress it. His hand shook as he lifted the brandy glass to his lips.

"What did the physician say, father?"

"What I knew he would say. That I am not long for this world. That some canker of the lungs is eating me away from the inside. It cannot be cured, or even slowed in its progress. I resisted taking laudanum for as long as I could, but now... the pain is too much without it. I... I have written, more than a week ago, and asked that Charles and Maria, and Hunter and Nerissa, come to Chester Park as soon as possible."

Kevin swallowed, emotion surging through him.

"Do you really expect to be gone from us so soon...?"

"I do. But do not talk of that, at least for now — tell me of Lady Hyacinth — do you love her? How did this betrothal come about?"

"If I am honest, it came about because I was uninspired by the ladies of the *ton*, filled with ennui, and beginning to wonder why I went to social events at all. So at the start of this season, I decided to study the people around me intensely, to determine whether there were any young women who were not dull. Lady Hyacinth — and her whole family, for that matter, is definitely not dull. She has a reputation for being sharp tongued and shrewish — but that is simply because most gentlemen cannot abide being told the truth by a woman."

Lord Chester laughed, and the laugh rapidly became a rasping cough. Kevin waited, allowing him the time to compose himself, before he went on.

"I decided that I would approach her, dance with her, simply because others didn't. For, surely, a woman with a reputation like hers would at least provide interesting conversation. And that she did. I became intrigued by her, completely. I think that I fell a little in love with her from our very first conversation. Which was delightfully blunt and refreshing. Over time, we began to see each other often – almost courting, without making it formal. Then, for no reason that I could determine, she became withdrawn and quiet, no longer offering her rather astringent and amusing comments on the people of the *ton* – comments which she had honoured me by sharing, when she usually kept those observations private."

"Oh? And what brought about that change?"

"Oddly enough, it was gossip, and the 'Gossip Gazette'. What I am about to tell you must go no further, but I believe that you will find it darkly amusing."

"My dear boy, of course it will go no further – it will go to the grave with me, and all too soon."

Lord Chester's laugh was self-deprecating, and Kevin admired his fortitude in the face of his illness. Yet he winced internally, at the reminder of his father's fragile mortality.

"Well… yes… you will remember, I hope, our conversations about the newssheet?" At his father's nod, he went on, "Well, it took me some little time to work it out, and connect what you had said, with what was happening, but I eventually did. For Lord Puglinton had threatened Lady Hyacinth."

"The bounder! But how had he done so?"

"Well… those sharp observations of society, which Lady Hyacinth had shared with me – she had generally only ever written them in a private journal. She did that, she told me, so that she could better prevent herself from making the observations directly to those they involved." Lord Chester laughed again, and coughed again. "What had happened, which allowed Lord Puglinton to threaten her, was that her journal had been lost – under circumstances which could, in a sense, be blamed on me. Puglinton found it, and began to publish her words in that scurrilous newssheet. At that stage, he had no idea who had written the journal, for it did not have her name in it."

"Then… how did he come to threaten her?"

"He worked it out. There was a very poor watercolour of a hyacinth flower in the journal, and he added that to her reputation for having a sharp tongue, to the fact that she had been present at all of the events which articles in the journal described, and concluded that it had to be her. He demanded that she either marry him, and write for him, or at minimum write for him, or he would expose her as the writer, which would destroy her reputation, and that of her sisters. And he implied that, even if she refused to marry him now, he might force her to it at any time, if she did not write enough, fast enough, to suit him."

"I knew that the man was unscrupulous, but I had never imagined he would take things that far."

"I hadn't either, until you gave me his name as associated with the 'Gossip Gazette' – then it all made sense."

"So… what have you done about it?"

"Well… the simplest way to protect Lady Hyacinth from him forcing her to marry him, was for her to be already married to someone else… and by then, the idea of marrying her had become very appealing, for the more time that I spent with her, the more I was coming to love her. But before I proposed, I wanted a solution to the whole problem – a way to remove his ability to blackmail her into writing for him. And you gave me that, when you told me of the suspicion that he had consistently cheated, when gambling, with the intent to ruin specific people."

"What did you do?"

"I concluded, although it did not sit so well with my principles, that the easiest way was going to be to blackmail the blackmailer. But that meant that I needed evidence of his wrongdoing. For that, I needed some assistance from Hunter's… associates… from his time in the military. They found what was needed, in a remarkably short time, assisted by that contact you had provided. Puglinton had been most careless with his correspondence in the past, most careless. And once confronted with that evidence, and the risk that it presented to his reputation and his fortune, he became most cooperative about returning the journal, and ceasing the publication of that column. We have those documents locked away, as a permanent bond for his good behaviour."

Lord Chester looked at his son, and a wide smile spread across his face.

"Whilst, of course, I cannot endorse blackmail… well done, Kevin, well done. So, once you held the evidence, you proposed?"

"I did, and she accepted me. I hope that you are happy with my choice, Father."

"I am, I am – I like the girl, sharp tongue and all. I prefer wit and opinion in a woman to insipidness. But... have the banns been read at all yet? How soon can you marry her? For I would fain see you married before I am gone." His speech was broken off by a fit of coughing, which resulted in an alarming amount of blood on the kerchief that he held to his mouth. His face had gone a frightening shade of grey. Kevin went to him, and clasped his hand on Lord Chester's shoulder, unsure of what he might do to ease his father's discomfort. Eventually, Lord Chester straightened in his chair, and sipped his brandy, then spoke. "And I not sure that I have the weeks to wait for the banns."

Kevin reached into his coat pocket, and withdrew the license. He unfolded it, and placed it on the desk before his father.

"Mother's letter did not explicitly address just how ill you have become, yet the sense of urgency it conveyed... I thought it best to take precautions. I am sure that both the Duchess of Elbury and Mother will adjust to the disappointment of having to act with speed, rather than pomp and ceremony, given the circumstances. Hyacinth does not know of this, yet, for I had hoped... but it seems that my hope for your improved health was very much in vain."

Lord Chester looked up at him, his face full of gratitude and pride.

"You will make a fine Viscount, my boy, there is no question of that."

"I will do my best to live up to your legacy, Father. But now, you should go to your bed and rest."

"I will, I will. Maria will be here tomorrow, as will Nerissa. If you speak to the vicar in the morning…"

"We can be wed the day after, with everyone who truly matters to us, present."

"Good, and thank you. I will go to God at peace, once I know that all of my children are wed and happy."

CHAPTER SIXTEEN

Hyacinth stepped into the church, which was lit by the golden glow of the summer morning sun, and filled with rainbows of light cast through the stained-glass windows. Kevin stood waiting for her, the deep reds in his hair accentuated by the coloured light. He had never seemed so handsome. As she walked towards him on her father's arm, a shiver ran through her. How different her life was, now, from just a few short months before, when she had faced the prospect of living out her life as a lonely spinster. Love filled her heart, and the only thing which cast any shadow on her happiness was the fact of Kevin's father's illness.

In the few days that she had known the man, she had become fond of him – his bluff cheerfulness, even in the face of the illness, was inspiring, and his love for his children was obvious. Hyacinth had readily agreed to the simple and rapid wedding – she had no need of grand ceremony, all that mattered was that she married the man she loved, whilst his father still lived to see it.

Her mother's disappointment had lasted a very short time – for she had the prospect of five more daughters to arrange weddings for – so one done in simplicity was not a great loss, especially when the reasons for it were so very important.

Hyacinth reached Kevin, and took his hand, standing beside him. The warmth of him reached her, and she felt cocooned in love. The vicar began to speak, and all thought of anything else fell away. Once the words were spoken, and it was done, a sense of unreality filled her. That her life could be changed so utterly, and so rapidly was astounding – and wonderful. They left the church, and were greeted by a shower of thrown flower petals, and a cheer from the inhabitants of the local village, who had come to see wed the man who would soon be their Lord.

As they stood in the sun, Lord Chester made his way slowly to them, using the cane that he now needed to walk, his breathing laboured and rasping.

"Welcome to my family, Lady Hyacinth. I hope that you will be happy, every day of your life. Thank you for agreeing to this rather rushed and quiet wedding, for my sake. I cannot express just how grateful I am."

Hyacinth stepped forward, and gently embraced Lord Chester. For a big man, he seemed surprisingly frail in her grasp, and sadness filled her, that illness had so reduced him.

"Thank you for being so welcoming."

He nodded, his eyes sparkling with unshed tears, and they all turned, moving slowly to the carriages which would take them back to Chester Park for the wedding breakfast – a relatively small affair of family, and some local nobility.

<<<< O >>>>

The ballroom at Chester Park had not seen so many people for quite some time. Given the short notice, quite a few people had been able to attend, and Hyacinth was attempting to keep all of their names straight in her mind. The minor nobility of the area did not often spend much time in London, and she had not met many of them before. They seemed an interesting enough collection of people, without the arrogance or fussiness of the *haute ton* in London.

The wedding breakfast was informally presented, with food laid out on long tables, and smaller tables scattered about the room, and on the terrace beyond the open French doors. Servants moved amongst them, ensuring that the guests were served whatever they wanted.

As a result, people mingled, and talked in a far more friendly way than Hyacinth had ever seen at a large gathering. Her sisters were, for once, not all together, but had each found themselves a different group of people to talk to. Hyacinth, seated beside Kevin, and his family, was content to simply watch everyone else, revelling in the knowledge that she was forever safe from Lord Puglinton, and that she had the rest of her life to explore her love for Kevin.

At a table not far from where she sat, Rose was engaged in conversation with two gentlemen – the Baron of Wrenton and his brother, if Hyacinth had remembered the introductions correctly. At the same table, Kevin's sister Maria, and her husband had joined the discussion. Snippets of what they were saying came to Hyacinth, half heard amidst the noise of other conversations. It had to do with food, and Hyacinth gave a little suppressed snort of laughter.

Of course it had to do with food – it was Rose, after all.

She wondered just what there was to discuss – food was food, as far as Hyacinth was concerned. But she heard the oddest things – they spoke of ice houses, and of storage, as well as of flour and more. How odd – for gentlemen were rarely interested in how food was produced. Perhaps they had business investments in mills or similar? Still, everyone seemed deeply engaged in the conversation, so Hyacinth shrugged – whatever made anyone happy seemed a good thing to her, in that moment.

She turned her attention back to Kevin and his parents, and proceeded to become caught up in their conversation – which was about Chester Park, and Lord Chester's hopes for its future with improved farming methods.

<<<< O >>>>

Kevin was acutely aware of Hyacinth beside him, for every second of the long day, from the moment that they were pronounced man and wife until the moment when, finally, they closed the bedroom door behind them, late in the evening. He drew her into his arms, and kissed her – a long slow kiss full of love, and passion. When they drew apart, he looked down at her.

"Thank you for being willing to stay here, rather than go on a wedding trip. I do not know how long my father has left..."

His throat closed on the words, and tears started in his eyes. He stared into Hyacinth's face, but the world blurred as the intensity of his emotions overcame him. She pulled him to her, and simply held him, as he finally allowed the sadness he had been holding back to surface.

"We will stay as long as we are needed. There is no reason to be anywhere else. I am glad that you were so clever as to have obtained the license before we left London, that we were able to do this for him, to have him there when we married."

Her fingers tangled in the hair at the nape of his neck, and she pulled him down to her again, bringing his lips to hers. The kiss was all that he had ever dreamed of, and so much more. He allowed it to warm the core of sadness inside him, allowed it to permit him to forget, for just a little while, what the next few days or weeks might bring. Whilst he held happiness in his arms, he would not allow himself to anticipate grief.

Gently, without breaking the kiss, he bent and lifted her, and carried her to the bed. Tomorrow would be soon enough to worry about everything else.

<<<< O >>>>

Three days later, Kevin was woken early by a loud wail. He started up in bed, shocked from deep sleep into immediate wakefulness. Beside him, Hyacinth opened sleepy eyes, and regarded him with confusion. Just as she opened her mouth to speak, another terrible wail rent the air.

They looked at each other, with horrified supposition in their faces. Without a word, they rose, and hastily dressed in the simplest of clothing, then rushed from the room. Another wail echoed down the hallways. It came, as Kevin had expected, from his father's room.

They raced in that direction, joining the crowd of others who emerged from rooms along the way. Once they reached the door, however, everyone stood back, and looked to Kevin. He took a deep breath, and opened the door.

His mother knelt beside the bed, wearing only her nightrail, and a wrap. She clutched his father's hand in hers, and her head rested on his chest. The wails came from her, interspersed with great racking sobs. Even from the doorway, Kevin could see that his father was not breathing. He lay, unnaturally still, his skin grey in the morning light, and the room was eerily silent, except for his mother's sobs. The heavy rasping which had been his father's breathing for so many weeks now was gone.

He went forward, slowly, as if in a dream. No amount of knowing that this day would come had prepared him for the reality of it. Grief clutched at his heart, and stole his breath. He was dimly aware that Hyacinth was beside him, but the entirety of his focus was on the bed, on his mother and father.

As if a spell had been broken when he crossed the threshold, his sisters rushed in behind him. Together, they gathered up their mother and held her, urging her gently from the room. As they almost carried her down the hallway, towards her small private parlour, Kevin heard Hyacinth speaking to the servants and the other guests who stood, unsure of what to do.

He heard mention of tea, and of calling the vicar, and the family in the village who performed the duties of undertaker for the area. Relieved, he turned his attention back to his mother, and to keeping his own grief at bay long enough to help her. It was as if the world was somehow distant from him, as if it should have stopped, as his father's life had stopped, yet it moved on around him, incomprehensibly.

He heard the servants reply to her – 'yes, Lady Chester' – and then it struck him, with the force of a punch to the head. He was now Viscount Chester, and Hyacinth was Lady Chester. His mother was now the Dowager Lady Chester.

In a corner of his mind, he laughed at himself, for feeling shocked – he had known all of this would come, had even discussed it with his father, these last weeks – yet it still seemed improbable, impossible, like a bad dream that he would surely wake from. Yet he knew it was not.

<<<< O >>>>

Hyacinth, observant as always, had taken in every detail at a glance, and understood the implications. She had taken a huge shuddering breath, as Kevin, Maria and Nerissa half carried their mother from the room, and had drawn herself up, forcing her mind to calm. Kevin was now Viscount Chester. Which made her Viscountess Chester. And, most importantly in that moment, made her the mistress of the house, and the one responsible for preventing things from falling into chaos.

The servants looked to her hopefully, their faces full of grief and confusion. Her own family looked to her, waiting for her to either take charge, or to ask for help. Hunter and Charles stood, torn between following their wives, and seeking some other way to help. Trembling, but determined, Hyacinth looked to the servants first. Ward, the butler, stood closest, next to Mrs Carson, the housekeeper.

"Ward, Mrs Carson – if you would ensure that all of the staff are informed, I would be most grateful. Please also arrange appropriate black armbands and other modifications to their attire, as well as whatever we will need to do around the house – send me the bills for whatever cost is incurred. Please ask Cook to send tea, and whatever small repast she thinks that the Dowager might be able to eat, to the Dowager's parlour. I believe that everyone else would be best served by retiring to the breakfast room at this point."

"Yes, Lady Chester."

The butler and housekeeper hurried off, chivvying the maids and footmen before them. Hunter stepped forward.

"The breakfast room?"

"Yes – we must all still eat, and we must consider everything that needs to be done. A list will be required. I do not know who the man of business used by this household is – I am assuming that whoever it is holds the most recent copies of the will? I will need help from everyone if all is to be done properly."

"I know the man of business, and his direction – I will deal with that."

Hunter's voice was steady, but his eyes drifted back towards the small parlour door, as if he wished to run to Nerissa's side as much as Hyacinth wanted to run to Kevin's.

"Thank you. Let us all move downstairs, and eat, whilst we work out what must be done."

They all turned, and did as she asked – returning to their rooms first, to dress appropriately for the day, in clothes at least partly suitable for mourning. As Hyacinth watched them go, she realised that she would need substantial additions to her wardrobe – for she had nothing really suited to mourning. Her father paused as he passed her, on his way back to the guest rooms. His hand came to rest on her shoulder, a quiet squeeze of reassurance.

"I am proud of you, daughter. Your strength and intelligence are most obvious today. You will manage to do it all, never fear."

She smiled and nodded, suddenly unable to speak – for if she did so, she feared that she would burst into tears.

He squeezed her shoulder again, then went on his way.

<<<< O >>>>

Kevin sat, Hyacinth's hand in his, as Mr Chedham rose from his seat and cleared his throat.

"We are gathered here for the reading of the last will and testament of James Loughbridge, Viscount Chester."

Everyone in the room stilled, watching him. Not that anyone expected anything unusual in the will, but still, such things had a gravity to them, a sense that surprise was still possible.

Mr Chedham unfolded the papers in his hand, adjusted his pince-nez on his nose, and began to read.

"To my son, Kevin, all things as appropriate and entailed to the title, for him to manage in trust for future generations. In addition to that, he shall also receive ownership of all of my business investments, funds, and all items not otherwise bequeathed in this will. To my wife, Eleanor, Belmont Cottage and its associated lands, and an annuity of ten thousand pounds, for as long as she may live. To my daughter Maria, the cottage on the Chester Park grounds, which she has always thought of as her own, to use in any way that she sees fit, and the monies in the bank account which I created as trustee for her. To my daughter Nerissa, the piece of land on the border of Chester Park and Meltonbrook Chase, which she has always loved, with my request that she turn it into a beautiful garden in my memory."

Small gasps and tiny expressions of half sadness, half amusement came with each bequest – for they were most appropriate to the people involved.

After the family, the list went on for some time, with bequests to various staff on the estates, and a few other people close to him.

There were only two surprises in the whole thing – a bequest to Charles and Maria of a property not far from their Northern estate – a property that none present had even realised that Lord Chester owned – and a codicil, added within the last few days of Lord Chester's life, which required that they be in formal mourning for no more than six months – no matter what society thought of it. Its wording made it clear that Lord Chester wanted his family to be happy, and to get on with their lives in his absence.

As they left the room afterwards, Kevin smiled, feeling his father's presence, as if he stood before him. He was more than grateful for that codicil – it was, he knew, his father's wedding gift to him, and Hyacinth.

EPILOGUE

Summer had moved on – it was early August, and most of the *ton* had retreated to their country estates. The Duke of Elbury however, was still in London, accompanied by his family. It had been a somewhat tumultuous year so far, with two weddings, and they had decided that staying in London was, perhaps, more desirable than the upheaval that came with removing them to the country.

This particular evening, they were joined by both of their now married daughters, and their husbands. Kevin and Hyacinth were dressed in sombre mourning clothes, for Kevin's father's death was but a few weeks past. It was only now that Kevin had felt comfortable leaving his mother to come to London. It had been necessary for him to deal with some business matters, and Hyacinth had taken the opportunity to accompany him, to see her family.

Lily and Trent were sitting with them, in the parlour, surrounded by the other Gardenbrook siblings. Earlier, Trent had taken Hyacinth aside for a moment.

His words had surprised her, at first, and then had made complete sense. He had said, simply – 'I do not believe that you are aware of the fact that I work with Baron Setford, at times. But I do believe that you understand what that means. Let me assure you that the right people are aware of Lord Puglinton, and the… agreement… that binds him. He will not trouble you again, I guarantee'. She had smiled, nodded, and whispered a thank you, and left it at that. But knowing that even more people watched over her well-being had lifted her spirits immeasurably.

Thorne had come into the room last, and now he looked around, his expression amused.

"So… now that both Lily and Hyacinth are wed, what can we expect next? The crown of family spinster now passes to Rose, and we will see what she can do to shed it, will we not?"

Rose fixed Thorne with a glare, and tilted her nose up.

"I am, most definitely, not a spinster! I am only twenty – that is a far cry from spinsterhood."

"Still, you must do something – follow the example set by Lily and Hyacinth – I am quite certain that you can find a man to suit you, if they could!"

Lily and Hyacinth both joined Rose in glaring at Thorne. Hyacinth turned to Lily, and asked, in her sweetest voice, "Should we take umbrage at Thorne's implication, on behalf of our husbands, do you think?"

Lily pretended to consider the question carefully, before nodding.

"I do think that we should."

Hyacinth turned back to Thorne.

"Well, brother, now that you have offended Lily and I, and our husbands, what will you do next? And what should we require of you, in reparation for your insults?"

"Reparation! Insult! My, but you do exaggerate, Hyacinth. Of course, I meant to say that Trent and Kevin have shown themselves to be gentleman of discernment, to have seen the value in you, when others could not. And I am, of course, quite certain that Rose will find an equally discerning gentleman."

Hyacinth snorted with laughter, amused at his careful wording. As she did, she glanced at Rose, who was, at this point, rather uncharacteristically silent. How interesting – did that mean that Rose actually had a gentleman in mind, perhaps? But Rose gave no indication, merely lifting a small cake to her lips and ostentatiously ignoring the entire exchange. Thoughtfully, Hyacinth responded, hoping to cause Rose to react.

"I, also, am quite sure that Rose will find a man who takes her fancy – all in her own good time, of course. He will need to be a man who cares about food, in all its subtleties – but I am certain that there must be one out there, somewhere."

Rose spluttered, and half choked on the cake.

"Really, Hyacinth, caring about food is not so unusual. And I mean about more than simply being a glutton. Why I met a man recently, who actually…"

She trailed off, suddenly realising that all other conversation had ceased, and that every one of her sisters had fixed her with a curious look. Hyacinth forced herself not to laugh at the consternation on Rose's face.

"Do go on, Rose – you met a man who…"

Thorne's voice was amused, and he smiled, waiting for her response.

"Nothing. Forget that I even mentioned it."

"My dear Rose, you know quite well that I have an impeccable memory – I could never forget a thing like that."

Rose glared at him. Hyacinth felt some sympathy for her, and decided to divert the conversation, a little.

"Rose… I have a suggestion – one which Thorne will, almost certainly, struggle with. You see, I, like Kevin, am required to wear mourning colours until January. And as, when you do eventually get married, I would truly prefer to attend in a colourful gown, rather than drab mourning colours, I do believe that gives you six months in which to find a man you like. So, my suggestion is this. Thorne agrees not to tease you, about spinsterhood, or finding a husband, for that six months, and, in that time, you do actually try to find a man you like… If, come January, nothing has happened, then Thorne will be free to tease you again."

Thorne spluttered a little in mock outrage.

"Hyacinth! You are cruel – how do you expect me to go a full six months without teasing Rose!"

"I am sure, my dear brother, that you are capable of such restraint. It will be good for your soul."

Rose looked at them both, and Hyacinth wondered what thoughts were passing behind her hazel eyes. After a moment, she nodded, and gave them a hard smile.

"Is that a challenge, Hyacinth? If so, I accept. Six months without Thorne teasing me will be a welcome respite. And perhaps, who knows, I will find a man I can care for..."

<<<< O >>>>

That night, as Kevin led Hyacinth to their bedchamber, he cast his mind back to the conversation in the parlour. It was so typical of Hyacinth's family – the good-natured teasing, which was underlaid by care. For he had seen what Hyacinth had done, with that last challenge to both Rose and Thorne – she had, most carefully, defended Rose, by ensuring that Thorne left her in peace, to chose her own path – at least for a few months.

It was so typical of Hyacinth, and what he loved about her – that aspect which he had noticed, right from the start – the kind heart, hidden behind the sharp toothed words, the tendency to care deeply for those she loved, and to defend them, tooth and claw, if needed, yet to do so in ways that were sheathed in subtlety.

As he had thought then, she was like a vixen – clever, cunning, able to hide in plain sight, and ferocious when defending her own. That he now ranked in that category was a delight and an honour – one he intended to be worthy of.

They reached their chambers, and entered, closing the door behind them. Hyacinth sighed, turning to him. As she spoke, he reached up to unpin her hair, enjoying the silken feel of it.

"I love my family, but really, sometimes... but I meant it when I said that I hoped that Rose found someone, and soon. I would not wish her to miss out on happiness, like this happiness we have."

He dropped the pins onto the bedside table, and turned his fingers to the matter of undoing her gown.

"Everyone should have this kind of happiness, my darling. And everyone should have a sharp toothed, sharp tongued vixen to defend them from the world."

She looked up, laughing, and he drew her into his arms to kiss her. She came willingly and they lost themselves in each other, and the delight of love found.

The End

I hope that you enjoyed
'A Vixen for a Viscount'

You'll find a taste of the next book
in the series,
'A Bluestocking for a Baron',
just after the 'About the Author'
section of this book.

ABOUT THE AUTHOR

Arietta Richmond has been a compulsive reader and writer all her life. Whilst her reading has covered an enormous range of topics, history has always fascinated her, and historical novels have been amongst her favourite reading.

She has written a wide range of work, from business articles and other non-fiction works (published under a pen name) but fiction has always been a major part of her life. Now, her Regency Historical Romance books are finally being released. The Derbyshire Set is comprised of 10 novels (8 released so far). The 'His Majesty's Hounds' series is comprised of 17 novels, with the last having just been released. The 'A Duke's Daughters – The Elbury Bouquet' series is comprised of seven books, with the second having just been released.

She also has a standalone longer novel shortly to be released, and four other series of novels in development. She lives in Australia, and when not reading or writing, likes to travel, and to see in person the places where history happened.

Be the first to know about it when Arietta's next book is released! Sign up to Arietta's newsletter at

http://www.ariettarichmond.com

When you do, you will receive two free subscriber exclusive books - **'A Gift of Love',** which is a prequel to the Derbyshire Set series, and ends on the day that 'The Earl's Unexpected Bride' begins, and **'Madame's Christmas Marquis'** which is an additional story in the His Majesty's Hounds series.

These stories are not for sale anywhere – they are absolutely exclusive to newsletter subscribers!

Connect with Arietta:

Follow her on Amazon - https://www.amazon.com/Arietta-Richmond/e/B016GG1KJ6/

Like her Facebook Page - https://www.facebook.com/AriettaRichmondAuthor

Follow her on Twitter - https://twitter.com/AriettaRichmond

Follow her on Instagram - https://www.instagram.com/AriettaRichmond/

Follow her on Bookbub – https://www.bookbub.com/authors/arietta-richmond

Follow her on Goodreads - https://www.goodreads.com/author/show/14508806.Arietta_Richmond

Here is your preview of

A BLUESTOCKING
FOR A BARON

A Duke's Daughters –
The Elbury Bouquet - Book 3
Clean Regency Romance

Arietta Richmond

CHAPTER ONE

Evan Shoreham, Baron of Wrenton, looked about the room, wondering why he had come. He did not know Lord Kevin well, and, whilst he had dealt with his father, Lord Chester, a few times, the family were barely acquaintances. Yet he had been invited to this wedding, and had felt, for some reason, the need to attend. Beside him, his brother, Hugh, nudged him.

"Choose somewhere to sit, Evan. We're blocking the doorway."

He moved into the room, and chose one of the scattered tables at random. The room filled up around him, and he watched as people filed in. Quite a gathering for this wedding breakfast, for their small part of the country. Not many he knew well, at all. As was inevitable, his attention turned to the long tables against the wall, where a large quantity of food was laid out, and servants waited to deliver it to guests, as required.

Food fascinated him. Not in the sense that he was a glutton, but in all other aspects — its provenance, preparation, and preservation.

Mentally, he catalogued the items present, assessing how much was seasonal, and easily available in the local area, and how much had to have been brought some distance, or preserved for some length of time. And how much might have been supplied through the vendors who used the ice houses that he owned.

Hugh sighed, obviously aware of where Evan was looking.

"Can you get your mind off business for a while, and actually celebrate the man's wedding, brother?"

Evan forced his eyes and mind away from the food tables, and turned back to the table he sat at. Opposite him, hazel eyes met his, from the most beautiful face that he had ever seen.

Everything else faded away but that face. Softly rounded, with rosebud pink lips set below a small nose, that face was impossible to look away from. Topped by wispy pale gold hair, which was determinedly escaping its pins, it was enchanting. He felt an intense urge to reach out and touch that soft hair.

He resisted, swallowing hard. At that moment, two other people sat down at the table. He forced his eyes away from that beautiful face to see who had just taken a seat. It was Lady Maria, Lord Kevin's sister, now Lady Wareham, and her new husband, Charles, Viscount Wareham. Maria smiled at him, and indicated him with her hand.

"May I present to you, Evan Shoreham, Baron of Wrenton, and his brother, Mr Hugh Shoreham. Gentlemen, this is Lady Rose Gardenbrook, a sister of the bride."

Evan swallowed, wetting his lips.

"Delighted, I'm sure."

It was all that he could manage to say. Beside him, Hugh nodded.

"I'm pleased to meet you, Lady Rose. Your sister looks truly the picture of a happy bride."

"Oh she is — very much so."

Lady Wareham smiled again, and looked at Evan.

"How are your business interests progressing, Lord Wrenton? I gather that some of the delicacies we have today, we would not have had without your ice houses?"

"That is true, Lady Wareham. Nearly all of the merchants who supply specialist foods in the area use them now. I am looking to expand, and add more locations."

"Wonderful! There are so many things that my mother particularly loves, which we could never get when I was a child."

Lady Rose made a little noise, and he turned back to her, caught again by her clear hazel eyes.

"You are in the business of ice houses, Lord Wrenton? How fascinating!"

Evan was shocked — fascinating was not a term that any woman had ever before used, with respect to his business. Generally, they were completely ignorant of the existence of ice houses, and had no wish to discover more.

"Errr, yes, I do find the whole process of preserving and storing food fascinating. That is what led me to investing in the business to begin with. My father thought me mad, then, but it has proven to be most profitable."

Hugh nodded beside him.

"Yes – at least our father saw that success, before he died. I think he was proud of what you'd achieved."

Evan paused a moment – their father had been gone two years now, but there was still a whisper of grief in him, when he thought too closely of the man.

Lady Rose regarded him a moment, a little hesitantly, as if making a choice, then she sat a little straighter, and spoke.

"My Lord, might I assume that you are following, with great interest, the research of those men who are attempting to create effective mechanical or chemical refrigeration techniques? If they succeed, the impact on food preservation will be enormous – think what you could do, with an ice house that did not require the collection of huge blocks of ice each year!"

Evan's head spun. This picture of feminine beauty before him knew about refrigeration research! And found it interesting! He must, of a certainty, be dreaming, for the improbability of it was beyond belief. But she was looking at him, waiting for an answer. He swallowed, hard.

"Yes, Lady Rose, I am very aware of it. I am hoping to invest at the first opportunity to create a commercial product from that research. That is, sadly, some years away, I believe. But the implications..."

"...are enormous. I can imagine a world in which all food can be kept far longer, in a far better state, and in which things that currently cannot be kept more than a day or so, might be preserved for weeks!"

Her eyes were bright, and her face animated.

Lady Wareham watched her with an expression of fond amusement. Apparently, Lady Rose was known to be rather a bluestocking on the matter of food related science, if that expression was anything to go by. But Lady Wareham then surprised him – she turned to him with a question of her own.

"Lord Wrenton, do you believe that such devices for refrigeration might one day be small enough to be installed in the larger homes, rather than being restricted to commercial ice houses? For I must admit that I would find such a thing most wonderful, for storing medicinal tisanes and possets."

"What a wonderful idea!"

Lady Rose positively beamed. Evan found himself smiling at her in return, completely captivated.

At that moment, a servant came to the table, carrying a plate of cream filled, pink iced, tiny cakes. He offered the plate to them, and Lady Rose reached out immediately to lift one from the plate, popping it into her mouth. She sighed – a sound of intense pleasure, closing her eyes for a second, and her tongue slipped out to lick the last of the icing from her lips. For an instant, Evan's imagination inserted that tongue, and that sound of pleasure, into an entirely different scene. Shocked at his response, he turned his eyes away from her. But the image was burned into his mind.

They allowed themselves to be distracted by food, as more was brought around, and the conversation shifted to more mundane things at times, but somehow, always kept coming back to his business plans. He permitted himself to indulge in the pleasure of speaking of his interests, with no need to simplify things.

The afternoon passed in the most pleasant conversation that he had enjoyed, ever. He was excessively glad that he had accepted the invitation to the wedding celebration. Lady Rose Gardenbrook was not only the most beautiful woman that he had ever met, she was the most intelligent, and intriguing. And she had exquisite taste in cakes.

<<<< O >>>>

The long summer twilight had slipped into evening, and still they sat, talking. Rose was in heaven. Finally, she had met a person who not only cared about the details of food, but who understood the technicalities of it all. A man who owned businesses which were dedicated to food. She had never had such a wonderful conversation in her life. And beside her, Maria had brought ideas to it as well – things that Rose had never considered, in the application of the same tools and preservation methods to medicines.

Her head spun. And, making it all the more perfect, the person involved was a man, not too many years older than her – a man so handsome that, when she had first seen him, it had quite taken her breath away. When she had arrived at the table with Charles and Maria, Lord Wrenton had been staring at the food tables, a small crease in his brow, as if he was puzzling something out. It had endeared him to her, instantly.

And everything had simply got better from there. When Maria had mentioned that his business was in ice houses, Rose had barely been able to conceal her excitement, and all thought of ladylike decorum had deserted her. It was only once she had asked him that question about refrigeration research, that she had paused, suddenly afraid that she had gone too far.

For, if a young lady showed too much interest in science, or studiousness in any way, she was like to be labelled a bluestocking, and avoided by the men of the *ton*. Rose had worked hard to avoid that label, by restricting her comments on any matters which might lead others to suspect just how much time she spent studying the things that intrigued her. Even her family were not completely aware of the depth of her interests.

Yet this man had, within moments of her meeting him, so disarmed her, and fascinated her, that she had forgotten all caution, and simply spoken. After her question, he had paused, and her heart had near stopped as she waited for his reaction – but then, he had answered her, seriously, with no sign of horror at the fact that a young woman even knew of such things.

From there, the conversation had become a thing of its own, and she had found herself finishing his sentences, and he hers, as they spoke of all of the remarkable discoveries of the last thirty years, and of the potential they held for the future. There were short pauses to eat, as various foods were brought around, and she had found his obvious conscious appreciation of the food as utterly intriguing as his intellect and scientific knowledge.

Now, the twilight sky slipped into the cobalt blue of evening, and they paused, as Maria yawned, then looked embarrassed.

"Oh, I am sorry! It is not that I find our conversation uninteresting – it is simply that I am most tired, after all of the preparations and the long day. And I do believe that most people have departed, or are preparing to do so. We have been so caught up that I had not noticed until now."

Rose looked around – it was true, few people remained.

Lord Wrenton and his brother rose from their seats, and the others followed their example. He came to Rose, and took her hand, bowing.

"Lady Rose, I can categorically say that this has been quite the most intriguing conversation of my life. Whilst we must take our leave now, and allow our hosts and their house guests their rest, I do hope that I might see you again, soon. For I would very much enjoy continuing this discussion."

His fingers had held her hand a little longer than was appropriate, and now they tightened a moment, before he released her. Her heart beat a thunderous tone, and her body seemed to have forgotten how to breathe for a moment. Then sense reasserted itself, and she drew a deep breath.

"Lord Wrenton, nothing would give me more pleasure. We will be staying here at Chester Park for at least a week – as you reside locally, perhaps we will have the opportunity to speak again, in that time."

"I will be certain to call, Lady Rose. Thank you, again, for a wonderful day."

Continued...

Read the rest of '**A Bluestocking for a Baron**' as soon as its released! Sign up for Arietta's newsletter at https://www.ariettarichmond.com to be the first to know.

BOOKS IN THE 'A DUKE'S DAUGHTERS – THE ELBURY BOUQUET' SERIES

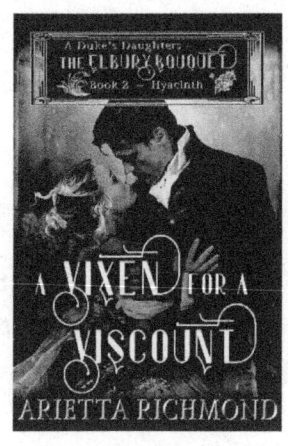

A Diamond for a Duke (Camellia)
(coming soon)
A Minx for a Merchant (Primrose)
(coming soon)
An Enchantress for an Earl (Violet)
(coming soon)
A Maiden for a Marquess (Iris)
(coming soon)
A Heart for an Heir (Thorne)
(coming soon)

BOOKS IN THE 'HIS MAJESTY'S HOUNDS' SERIES

BOOKS IN 'THE DERBYSHIRE SET'

The Earl's Unexpected Bride

The Captain's Compromised Heiress

The Viscount's Unsuitable Affair

The Count's Impetuous Seduction

The Rake's Unlikely Redemption

The Marquess' Scandalous Mistress

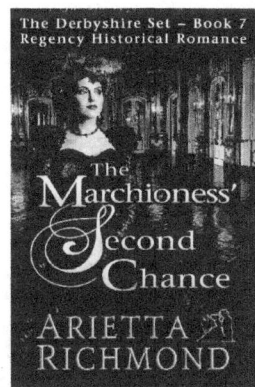 

The Marchioness' Second Chance

Lady Theodora's Christmas Wish

The Derbyshire Set Omnibus Edition Vol. 1 (the first three books all in one)

The Derbyshire Set Omnibus Edition Vol. 2 (the second three books all in one)

Available at all good book stores and for ebook readers too!

REGENCY COLLECTIONS WITH OTHER AUTHORS

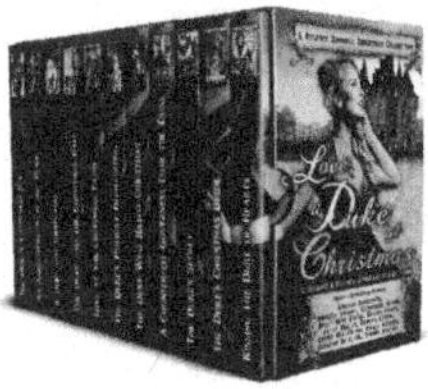

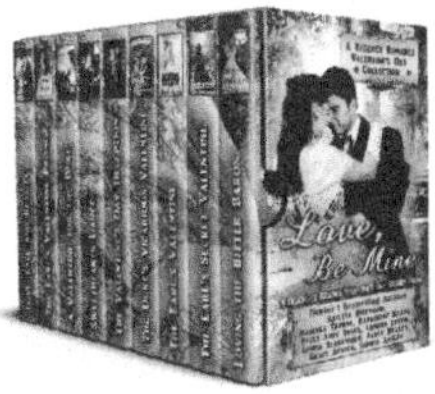
Love, Be Mine

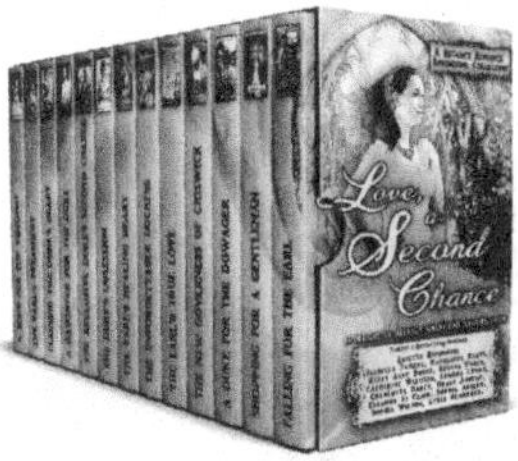
Love, a Second Chance
A Duke for the Dowager
Falling for the Earl

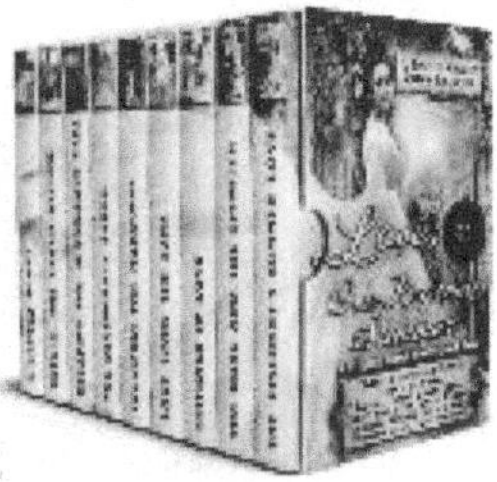

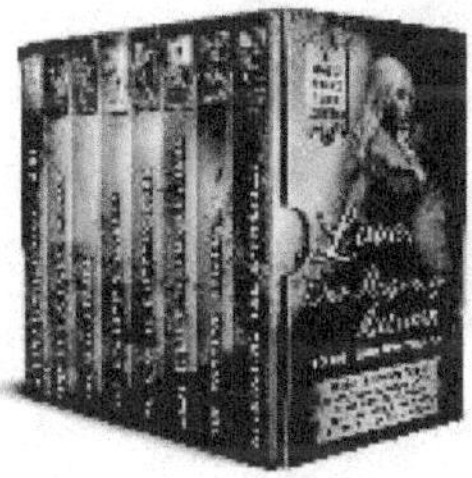

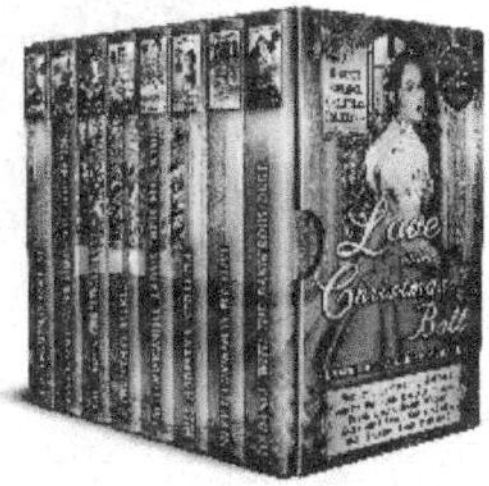

The Duke's Outrageous Daughter
The Perfect Second Chance
Capturing the Earl's Heart
The Duke Claims His Lady
To Woo a Lady
A Spinster for a Spy

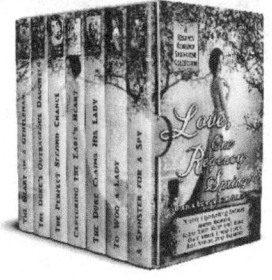

BOOKS IN THE
NETTLEFOLD CHRONICLES

OTHER BOOKS FROM
DREAMSTONE PUBLISHING

Dreamstone publishes books in a wide variety of categories, ranging from Erotica and Romance to Kids Books, Books on Writing, Business Books, Photography, Cook Books, Diaries, Colouring books and much more. New books are released each month.

Be the first to know when our next books are coming out

Be first to get all the news – sign up for our newsletter at

http://www.dreamstonepublishing.com

37123707R00118